BROKEN
BRIDE

BROKEN SERIES BOOK ONE

paige press

BROKEN BRIDE

BROKEN SERIES BOOK ONE

STELLA GRAY

Paige Press
Leander, TX 78641

Ebook:
ISBN: 978-1-953520-54-8

Print:
ISBN: 978-1-953520-55-5

Editing: Erica Russikoff at Erica Edits
Proofing: Michele Ficht

ALSO BY STELLA GRAY

The Bellanti Brothers

Dante

Broken Bride

Broken Vow

Broken Trust

ABOUT THIS BOOK

*I was sold to him to settle a debt... but Dante Bellanti
never settles.*

My father was always a gambling man.
Unfortunately, he never could pick winners.
When the wolves closed in, he chose himself, like always.

He traded his freedom... for mine.

He forced me to marry.
Now Dante Bellanti owns my body.
I'm just another possession for a man who already has too
much.
So I won't let him have my heart.

But you know what they say about gambling.

The house always wins.

And I'm at the mercy of the Bellantis...

PROLOGUE
DANTE

Iт's a proper day for a funeral.

Storm clouds gather overhead, dark and looming, but not a single drop of rain dares to fall on the last party that Enzo Bellanti will ever throw. All eyes swivel toward me as I step outside the doors of St. Helena's, where black-clad mourners crowd the courtyard.

I'm tall, broad in the chest and shoulders, slim in the waist and hips, wearing a perfectly tailored pinstripe Kiton suit. My style and stature is familiar to the guests, the outline of Enzo's eldest offspring giving them the impression that I'm *him*...that perhaps my father isn't really dead after all.

My face is granite as I meet their serious gazes, seeing the calculation there. The big question on everyone's mind: *What's going to happen to the Bellanti family now?*

A heartbeat passes and then the spell breaks, the mourners returning to their hushed conversations. The sea of black—women in midnight dresses and hats with

1

charcoal feathers and netting, the men in proper mourning suits and fedoras—matches the sky. And my mood.

Behind me stand my younger brothers, Armani and Marco, equally turned out and equally imposing.

The wind picks up, and I take a deep breath and gesture the grieving masses inside.

It's time.

Standing by the door as everyone streams past, I nod my head and utter quiet thanks as people murmur their condolences. Most of them I've known since I was a child. Some are new to me, though I know their backgrounds. I've read their files. I know what their dealings with my father were. Their faces all wear similar masks of concern, though it doesn't escape me that each and every one of them wants something from me. A continuation of their business with my father. A resolution. A comforting word. Advice.

Maybe a favor.

Favors are what my father traded in, and half the people here owe the Bellantis money (or more) in return. With him gone, it's my job to settle the books. Cash in and move the family forward. It's going to take some effort to sort things out, dig into the nitty gritty of who owes what, but I will. Down to the last detail. And I'll collect in full. The expressions of everyone brushing by me show that they know it, too.

Once the mourners are all inside, I turn to check on my younger brothers.

Armani is slightly taller than me but more slender,

decked out in his own bespoke suit. He's wearing his neutral face, the one that makes him damn hard to read, but I know he's doing everything he can to keep it together. Marco, the youngest of us, has on his trademark scowl. His hair is slicked straight back, glossy in the natural light like a television mobster. He cuts me a look, then tosses a nod in the direction of the pews.

I nod back.

Armani waits for me to pass and takes up the rear after closing the doors.

We sit up front, but I can't tell how much of the service my brothers absorb. I hear the words, the mass, the hymns, the prayers, but it filters right through my mind and straight out. There's so much to be done now that he's gone.

Soon the mass is complete, the speeches over, the tears—both real and fake—shed. After pallbearing, we climb into the back of a black armored car with bullet-proof glass and lead the procession of vehicles to the cemetery. Once we're there, my brothers and I all file out into the gloom once again and make our way graveside.

I'm numb. Or, no—I'm somewhere else entirely. Body standing there in the grass, listening to the dirt hit the casket, while my mind is a million miles away.

Burial done, the three of us are left staring at the mound of earth that now covers our once formidable father.

Guests take their leave, some lingering in the background to talk. Marco is about to say something when a tight little blonde weaves her way into our trio with an apologetic smile and rests a hand on his forearm. She's in a black bodycon dress and heavy makeup that's more appropriate for a club, but I'm not surprised. It's how Marco prefers his women: all flash. He's still working his way through all the pussy in town like it's his job. Who am I to rein him in…yet?

He moves off with her, leaving me and Armani alone. I'm glad we'll have the chance to talk privately. I exhale, and it feels like the first time in hours.

My brother sinks his hands into the pockets of his pants and pulls his gaze from the grave to me. "The Bruno family representative was here."

"I noticed." I frown. The Brunos are a SoCal crime syndicate who've been looking to expand into Northern California. "What'd he say?"

"They're eager to buy out our notes. Snap up their own slice of the gambling pie before the Chows in San Francisco muscle in."

"I'm open to that," I say.

The truth is, I'd be glad to get rid of those notes. I'd already begun scouring through my father's holdings, weeding out the bad gambling debts we need to collect. My father had no qualms about loaning unlucky gamblers money to feed their habit, but I find it distasteful to prey on addicts.

Beyond that, collecting the note and interest was and always will be a cat and mouse game of how much violence it takes to force a borrower to pay up—and I'm not one for violence. If I have to exert some muscle, I prefer it be against someone who actually deserves it. Not some poor schmuck with an addiction to the ponies.

"Well, it's off your plate then," Armani says. "I'll have the books turned over to the Brunos by the end of the month. Including some of our staff who'll want to stay on under the new management."

I raise my chin in acknowledgement, but I can tell my brother isn't done yet. "What else?"

"We still have a few other loose ends to tie up." Armani looks away and clears his throat. "Including the Abbotts."

My shoulders tense. "Leave them to me."

"But we were gonna write that off with the rest of the—"

"I said I'll take care of it." I slice my brother a look, silencing him. "You can handle the rest, but keep the Abbott debt out of the deal with the Brunos. I'm dealing with the Abbotts myself."

Our father's gone. I'm in charge now.

This is one account no one else is going to touch.

FRANKIE

Napa Valley. Gosh, it's good to be home.

Gentle hills roll around me as I drink in the sights from the back seat of the town car, the distant rows of grapevines lush and green against a lemon drop and tangerine sky. The three years I've been gone have flown by, and now that I'm in the welcoming arms of my hometown, it seems almost impossible to believe I'd ever left. My time in Tuscany had been crucial to the future success of our family winery, and I'm glad that I went—I'd go again in a heartbeat—but now I'm ready to get my fill of my family and my home.

Olivia and Charlotte have been texting nonstop since I landed in Oakland, asking for my ETA and sending endless celebratory and heart-shaped emojis. Though my sisters flew out to Italy to visit me a few years ago, I can't wait to see them again. Livvie turned eighteen while I was away, and Charlie had run off and eloped. Thank goodness for social media so I could keep up with them.

Life really does go on when you're not around, and I clung to every Insta picture they dropped to help me feel like I was still a part of their journeys.

The landscape changes gently as we take the familiar route to our winery. My face is close to the window, my breath fogging the glass. Napa is amazingly similar to Italy—the ordered rows of vines, the commanding vistas, even the architecture of some of the homes are similar— but there's something about Napa that's completely its own. Maybe it's the unique blend of sprawling estates and down-home mom-and-pop places.

The flash of a red and yellow sign up ahead catches my eye and I ask the driver to slow down. The Alvarez fruit stand has been here as long as I can remember, but as we approach, I find it's very different from when I left.

"Can you pull over, please? I'll just be a few minutes. You can keep the meter running."

"No need," the driver says with a smile. "I'm happy to take a break and get a bite to eat here. Twenty minutes enough time for you?"

"Yes, thank you!"

The car is barely stopped as I open my door and slip out.

Beneath my feet, the hard packed dirt is familiar, along with the sweet and earthy scent of fresh produce. The stand used to consist of a few tables inside an open-face, three-walled shed. Now, it's been replaced with a much larger enclosure, a pavilion with pink and orange bougainvillea trellising up the poles. I see heaps of fruits and vegetables on display, a cluster of picnic tables, even a gazebo off to the side. A pebble walkway invites guests to wander as they enjoy their treats, while overflowing pots of geraniums and fuchsia hang from tall shepherd's hooks around the property.

My chest swells as I spot a familiar figure inside the stand. The woman turns as if she knows I'm here, and calls to me before I can beat her to it.

"Frankie Abbott, back from Italy!"

Delores Alvarez comes toward me with open arms, wrapping me in her comforting embrace and giving me the kind of squeeze that used to crush the wind out of me when I was small. I always loved it, though. I still love it now. She was one of my childhood heroes.

"Hi, Mrs. Alvarez."

She holds me at arms' length and gives me a sly smile and a once-over. "Oh, Frankie. Tuscany suited you. Look at that tan skin and that sun-kissed blonde hair. So pretty. Even more than usual."

Heat flares in my cheeks the way it does whenever someone compliments me. "Thank you. I love what you've done with the place! When did all this happen?"

"Come on, I'll give you the tour."

She shows me the pavilion and the gazebo, and then we wander through the fruit stand to the back room. Nostalgia hits me as I enter. The building may have been expanded, but this room is exactly the same. Shelves piled high with carefully labeled boxes. Produce crates stacked in the corner. Signs on silver metal stakes set against the wall. The air is heavy with the scents of cinnamon horchata, fresh strawberries, and citrus.

"Sit, Frankie, sit." Mrs. Alvarez waves to the same café table and set of chairs I sat at as a child. I spent many happy afternoon hours in this back room, assembling boxes of produce, making fruit cups with chili pepper, lime juice, and sea salt, and learning the ins and outs of running a thriving business.

As a longtime family friend, Delores always had time for me when my father didn't, and never once complained when he'd drop me off while he went to run errands. I loved the hustle and bustle of customers lining up to buy groceries or grab a homemade treat. I learned how to interact with customers, how to be charming and unafraid to interact with the public. The hard work and tight margins of running a family business didn't get past me, either. I took it all to heart and I have Delores to thank for the businesswoman I am today.

One who hopes it's not too late to turn my family's winery around.

"How about a snack?"

"I'd love one," I say. "My driver's waiting for me though, so it has to be a quick one."

Delores moves to the worktable and quickly scoops slices of cantaloupe, jicama, papaya, mango, and watermelon into plastic cups before spicing them with a generous dash of classic chili-lime salt. Then she pours a steaming cup of dark roast for us both and joins me across the intimate, round table.

"Cheers!" She clinks her cup of fruit against mine.

I pop a piece of cantaloupe into my mouth and moan at the blend of sweet and spicy. Talk about childhood memories. I have a mild out of body experience with the first few bites, then realize Delores is rapidly catching me up on all the local news and gossip that I've missed.

She's an expert summarizer, and quickly rattles off three years' worth of happenings. I try to keep up as she explains in her signature animated hand gestures and whispered, "who done it" tone about the new babies, the hookups, the breakups, whose kids went off to college. Divorces. Marriages.

"How's Mama Alvarez?" I ask. She's the matriarch of their family.

Mrs. Alvarez grins. "Retired, and still kicking. She had a hip replacement last year but she's as spry as ever."

"Glad to hear it," I say.

"Oooh, and you heard, I'm sure, that Enzo Bellanti died."

My sister texted me about it shortly after the news went public. I nod. "I heard."

Mrs. Alvarez makes an exasperated sound and shakes her head. "You know, he was the one who loaned us the money to build the pavilion. At a reasonable rate, too. He knew we'd repay him someday."

A chill whispers over my skin, as if a cool breeze suddenly touched me.

"A lotta folks in Napa owe the Bellantis favors like that," she goes on. "Just like—"

Her voice trails off and the chill washes over me again. "Just like what?"

Delores sets her cup down, looking guilty. "I don't want to gossip about your family, Frankie. But it's no secret that your father owes a lot of people. Both local and out-of-town. You haven't been home in so long, but... do you know what's happening over there? Your father's missed deliveries around town, and the place is rarely open to visitors or tour groups anymore. The Abbott Winery's doors are all but closed."

The papaya in my mouth might as well be a cold chunk of coal. I set down my fruit, take a careful swig of coffee, and paint on a smile. I know all about my father's financial shortcomings, thanks to my sisters and their frantic, sometimes daily messages over what's been going on. The Recession hit us hard back in '08, when us kids were too little to understand what was going on, and my family has been struggling to get out of the red ever since.

Now, it seems that our father has given up.

As for me, I think the Abbott Winery is simply going through a rebuilding stage. Going to Italy to learn how to grow and evolve a winery was just one tool in my repair kit to bail out the family business. I'd hoped to get a jump on things before gossip about our debts leaked, but it seems like I'm too late.

Who else knows?

Forcing another smile, I rise and smooth my hands down my thighs. "Thank you so much, Mrs. Alvarez. I really need to get going, though. I can't wait to see my sisters."

She envelops me in another generous hug, and I depart with the promise to be back soon. Once I'm back in the car, I instruct my dad's driver to continue on to the winery.

Some of my joy at being home has diminished with the thought that my family's business has deteriorated to the point that it's becoming the whisper of the town. We finally turn onto the gravel road that cuts through the vineyards and leads to the house, and our property is both familiar and foreign to me. The vines are vibrant in their full summer growth, but they hang in overgrown clumps along their supports. Untrimmed, untended. My heart sinks as I spy bunches of grapes touching the ground here and there, left to lay and rot.

My throat goes tight as we reach the main winery compound. It's the epicenter of our winery and should be bustling with visitors tasting our wines and socializing while tipsily nibbling from charcuterie boards and tapas plates.

But it's empty. Completely empty.

Mrs. Alvarez warned me, but it's still a shock.

I'd been so excited to see my sisters, but I push that aside now as desperation and disbelief pressurize inside my gut. I pay the driver, grab my bags, and rush up the stone path to the house. Some of the anxiety lessens as I notice how well the exterior of the house and grounds have been maintained. The lawn is tidy, flowers in full bloom.

But when I swing open the door and step inside, I notice immediately that the tulip-laden Dutch Golden Age painting that my family cherished for generations isn't hanging in its coveted spot just inside the entry where guests couldn't help but notice it.

Now, an off-color square covers the wall where the

framed artwork protected the paint from sunlight and aging over so many years.

"Dad?" I call out, dropping my bags in the entry as I make my way through the house.

The formal dining room to the left yawns emptily as I pass. The French dining room set that was gifted to my grandfather from a winemaker friend in Beaujolais, who beautifully colored the wood with stain made from his own grapes, is gone. I skid to a stop and do a double take. My heart stutters as I rush to the living room. There, a cheap coffee table and chairs replace the rich leather ensemble that once comfortably filled the room. The Turkish hallway runner leading to the staircase is missing, too.

Evidence of my father's debts.

I run to his den, not bothering to knock as I yell, "Dad!" and throw open the door.

He's stretched out on the sofa, his feet propped up on the armrest. There's a beer in one hand, and the other is pumping the air as he yells at a baseball game on the small flatscreen in the corner.

"Dad." I hurry to him, my heart pounding. He shakes his head at the TV and takes a swig of his beer, not bothering to look at me. My brow furrows. "What is going on around here?"

"The A's are screwing the whole season, that's what's going on," he says, not even bothering to stand up and greet the daughter he hasn't seen in three years.

Anger surges through me. This isn't exactly the welcome I expected. My father isn't a warm, loving man by any stretch, but this cold brushoff is stringent, even for him.

"Excuse me," I say, crossing the room to stand in front of the TV. "But where is the furniture? And where are all the guests? The winery looks like it's closed—"

"It is closed." He takes another swig of beer as my stomach twists in knots.

"W-why?"

"It's temporary, girl. Settle down. And please don't block the tube. It's the last inning."

Stepping aside, I run a hand through my hair and grapple to get my emotions under control. My sisters had hinted that things were falling apart around here, but I'd thought they were being a little dramatic. This vineyard is our legacy. Dad wouldn't let it just fall apart.

"Dad, please. The vines are a mess. How can you close the doors on the one thing that makes us money?"

That at least gets him sitting up and looking my way. "You watch yourself, Frankie."

"This is our legacy," I protest. "Don't you care even a little bit what happens to this place?"

The corner of his hard mouth pulls up and I can't tell if it's a smile or a smirk. "Of course I care. But I got it all figured out. So quit your worrying."

He turns his attention back to the game, and suddenly I feel a chill.

"What do you mean you *got it all figured out*?" I ask.

Without even glancing over, he says, "I sold the vineyard to the Bellantis."

He says it so casually that I fear I'm hallucinating it,

but as I process his words, my heart drops. My lips part, but I struggle to speak. I can't comprehend this.

"You can't do that to us. Why did I even go to Italy to learn if you're just going to sell the winery out from under us?"

"Like I said, you can quit your worrying." He turns the volume up higher. "All that hard learning you did will be put to good use after all. You're part of the package."

I'm struggling to keep up. "What does that mean?"

"Contract's already signed. You're gonna marry the heir."

FRANKIE

You're gonna marry the heir.

Just like that? I've been...sold? I can't believe what I'm hearing.

"What the hell are you talking about?"

My body buzzes with nervous energy, pent up and vicious, and I act by rote as I storm over and grab the remote from him. Then I turn off the TV and throw the remote across the room, where it hits the floor and spits batteries. He doesn't have the grace to look a bit phased.

"What did you just say?" I demand.

My dad looks to the ceiling and crosses his work-hardened hands over his middle. "Settle down. You always said you wanted to marry young, Frankie. Here's your chance. You're going to be so damn rich you can honeymoon around the world if you want."

I gape at him. Marry young. The words feel like a slap in the face. The memory of soft brown eyes and strong hands holding me tight threatens to overwhelm me on the spot. Young love. My one chance...gone but never forgotten... And now this.

The cold, hard reality of the situation has me grinding out my words. "You sold me off like *cattle*."

Dad shrugs. "Why are you acting like I auctioned you off? You should be thanking me."

"Thanking you? You're insane. I will not be going through with this. I do not consent."

"You think I need your consent, girl? I don't."

"What do you think this is, Dad, the Dark Ages? I won't do it."

Suddenly the door flies open. My older sister Charlie cries my name and grabs me in a bear hug from behind. My body is stiff as stone and her excited voice makes a sharp drop as she spins me around. She's exactly as I remember her, tall and willowy, with a few adorable premature laugh lines around her eyes from the permanent smile she's always sporting. It's not often I see my sister without that smile, in fact—though it's fading fast as she searches my face.

God, I'd been so excited to see her after all this time, but now...I can't think straight.

Her jaw works to one side as she picks up on the tension in the room. A frown crosses her smooth face; a typical reaction when my father is around.

"What have you done, Dad?" she says, shooting him a glare.

He doesn't respond.

"Frankie?" Her voice is small. "What happened?"

I attempt words. Fail. Attempt again and they squeak

out. "Dad sold the winery to the Bellantis. He just informed me that I'm part of the purchase contract. I'm supposed to marry the Bellanti heir."

Charlie bursts out in an incredulous laugh, but there's no humor in her eyes as she looks at our father over my shoulder. "Is this some kind of 'welcome Frankie home' joke? Because I'm not in on it. Are there hidden cameras, or—" Her voice trails off. She shifts uncomfortably.

"It's no joke." Dad sighs as if he's bored with this whole thing.

"*Marry the heir?*" Charlie repeats, horrified. "Sold the...what are you talking about?"

I mirror my sister's stance as we both stare down our father, but I'm numb all over. My existence feels surreal. Dad speaks, and Charlie responds. I don't comprehend either of them.

My future was decided without any input from me. While I was working my ass off in Italy, learning everything I possibly could in order to make my family business better, my father was plotting his exit and tossing me to the wolves. He's completely dismissed the effort I put into learning how to better the winery. Instead, I've become a commodity.

"Why would you agree to this, Dad? You always say the Bellantis are assholes!" Charlie's shouting now, hands clenched into fists at her sides. "Look, let's put the winery aside for a minute and focus on the bigger issue. You tossed your own daughter into the bill of sale like she's not even a *person*. You think Frankie's your property or something? There's no way she's going through with it!"

Charlie's cheeks are stained red, her eyes glassy with a fury I can't recall ever seeing her exhibit before. Her famous smile? So far away, I can barely recall what it looks like. Dad steeples his fingers and leans back on the couch. He doesn't look ashamed. Annoyed, maybe.

"It was either Frankie or Livvie," he finally blurts. "And we all know Livvie would never survive a man like Dante Bellanti."

"*What?*" Charlie gasps.

Dad looks away from us, out the window, maybe in an attempt to dismiss us. Maybe to avoid our seeing whatever emotion might be playing on his face. Though truthfully, he's never been the emotional type.

As for me? I have enough emotion for all of us as I imagine my sweet, innocent baby sister being thrown to the Bellantis like chum to sharks. "This can't be happening," I murmur.

"I was in pretty deep, so they said I had to pay deep," Dad goes on. "Their terms were nonnegotiable: they wanted one of you as a bride along with the vineyard. If I didn't agree, they'd take one of you to the grave...and then they'd still get the vineyard."

Charlie's jaw has dropped, and both of us are shocked and silent.

Dad clears his throat as he leaves the couch long enough to pick up the remote from the floor, get the batteries back into it, and click the television back on. "You'll meet him and it'll be fine, Frankie. You'll see."

I shake my head. "But—"

"It'll be *fine*," Dad repeats. He settles into the couch, eyes back on the television.

A wave of dizziness crashes over me. Charlie's arms are suddenly around me and she's leading me from the room. Arm in arm, we head upstairs to my old bedroom, leaving the den and our shitty father behind.

Charlie eases me down onto the bed and smooths my hair back. Then she sits next to me and starts rubbing my back in slow circles. I'm breathing hard, as if I just ran around the vineyard with our yellow Lab, Penelope. She passed away while I was in Italy, and I'd give anything to be able to wrap my arms around her soft fur now and let her tuck her sweet head under my chin. My sisters and I used to joke that Penny was the fourth Abbott sister.

"Shh," Charlie whispers softly. "It'll be okay."

"I'm not marrying into the mob." My voice is shaking. "But...they'll kill one of us."

Giving voice to the words cements them somehow. This is real. There's no backing out of a deal with the Bellantis—and they don't make empty threats. Not ever. They're one of the oldest mob families in this area. Everyone is indebted to them. Everyone.

I can't hold it in any longer, and I collapse against Charlie's shoulder and start to sob.

"I don't want to get married," I wail. "And if I did, it wouldn't be to a cold, calculating control freak like Dante Bellanti. I'll be nothing but a trophy to him."

Or worse. A prisoner.

My sister rocks me for a bit, until I finally calm down

enough to get a few tissues and dry my eyes. Then I sink back onto the bed, still dazed and now with a fresh headache.

"Listen," Charlie says. "Maybe it won't be so bad. You know? You'll be protected, and set for life, with everything you need or want. I know it's not what you've always dreamed of, but it could turn out okay. Marrying into a Family isn't the worst thing."

If I didn't know what Charlie's been through, I might find her attempt at consoling me slightly infuriating. But she married a made man herself. She's already walked a similar road.

"Our life together is relatively peaceful," she continues. "He heads out in his suit every morning after we have coffee together, and then sometimes he's out of town for a few days, but for all intents and purposes he's just another high-powered businessman who keeps long hours. I just don't ask about his work. Ever."

Imagining myself going through the motions like that has me breaking down all over again. I swipe at my tears, trying to catch my breath, when I hear footsteps in the hall outside.

Before I can run for the en suite, the bedroom door bursts open.

"Frankie!"

Our youngest sister Olivia, all bubbles and squeals and happiness, bounces onto the bed and wraps us both in a bear hug. Her fruity floral perfume washes over me and I remember poring over her sunny social media posts. Her sweet face, her youthful innocence.

She leans back, her pale blonde brows drawn together. "Why are you crying?"

Forcing a smile, I lie, "I'm just happy to be home."

And just like that, there's no doubt in my mind.

I pull her into my arms again.

Charlie runs a hand protectively down Livvie's hair. I catch my older sister's eyes and nod slightly, just enough that she knows. Dad was right—it has to be me. Not Livvie. I couldn't live with myself if I let her marry Dante.

I have to do this for our family.

"Guess what else, Liv?" I almost choke but I hold it together. "I'm getting married."

3

FRANKIE

Yᴇᴀʜ, this isn't going to cut it.

The Versace dress I'm holding against my body is designer, but it's four years old and solid black...not really my color. Unfortunately, it'll have to do. The moment my father informed me I was engaged, the ball started rolling —and now I'm on a ride I can't get off of. Apparently, I have a formal dinner tonight to meet my fiancé, just him and me. Alone.

I'm not good with spontaneity and surprises. I prefer having things laid out before me in advance, in black and white, so I know exactly what to expect. Which is why, having never met Dante in person before, I've decided to go to the Bellantis' winery today and introduce myself to my fiancé ahead of time. My hope is that it will ease some of the apprehension and awkwardness between us at the formal dinner later. For all I know, he's nervous about this arrangement, too. Breaking the ice might be good for both of us.

Problem is, my wardrobe is seriously lacking. This in Napa Valley, after all. And I'm about to be the wife of a mob boss and a member of an incredibly wealthy winery family. I should be dressed to fit the image. But I didn't need designer clothes while I was in Italy, so my suitcase is stuffed with nothing except faded denim and worn-out button-downs. Fashion isn't much of a concern when you're spending long hours physically working in a vineyard or behind the scenes with your sleeves rolled up.

"Here you go!" Livvie trills, popping into my room with my heels outstretched. I do a double take. I can't believe they're the same dull, scuffed Manolos I gave her just a few minutes ago. She managed to polish the black leather to a brilliant shine. Not a scuff to be seen. They're actually presentable again.

"This is amazing, Liv. Thank you."

"We're not done yet. Sit."

She takes the dress from me and lays it on the bed before pushing me onto the stool in front of my mirror. After a moment's disappearance, she comes back with a silver tackle box-looking container and spreads it open on the vanity.

I raise my eyebrows. "Good lord. That's a whole arsenal."

She smiles proudly and fiddles with the haul of cosmetics and various beauty tools arranged in the trays. "I may have a small makeup problem."

"Well, you don't need any of it," I tease her. "You're a natural beauty."

"Yeah, but it's fun to play with." She shrugs with a

clearly pleased smile. "Okay, keep your face soft. No frowning. No smiling. Just relax those muscles."

She pokes at my cheek...pokes again until I relax my face. I sit quietly as she works her magic. Livvie has the gift of gab, and it's out full force as she layers on the eyeshadow and sweeps highlighter over the rise of my cheekbones.

"I'm so tickled that I'm going to be your bridesmaid!" She lifts my chin. "You should totally let me pick out the dresses. Nothing strapless, of course, and I'll be subtle with the color."

"I haven't given it much thought yet, Liv. This all happened so fast."

"Oh I know, but really, you should let me just do it. I've got a couple ideas in mind already."

Bridesmaids. Dresses. Wedding planning.

My chest constricts. It's been less than twenty-four hours since I found out I'm about to have a husband, and I can't bring myself to acknowledge anything related to the wedding. I just want to meet this man and get the initial awkwardness out of the way. Besides, what's the point of planning a wedding you don't even want? I hold my left hand out before me. There's no ring, either. What kind of engagement doesn't have a ring?

There was a time when I'd imagined my perfect wedding and my perfect groom. Dreamed about rose petal-strewn aisles, embroidered ivory dresses, arched arbors dripping with a mix of grapevines and mustard flowers as a nod to the winery, along with fat pink peonies and sprays of ferns and eucalyptus. The ceremony would take place in our vineyard at sunset so everyone could dance afterward under the live oaks strung with fairy lights.

But that was a long time ago, and some things aren't meant to be.

"You should wear your hair down tonight," Livvie chatters. "I'm going to curl the ends, give you some bounce. You've got all these stunning highlights from the sun. Italy must be really sunny, huh? It looks like you had these done in a salon. They're just so perfect."

She finally takes a breath, waiting, and I realize I didn't respond.

"Oh, yes. It's sunny. Even in the winter, when it drops to the forties sometimes."

"Well it worked for you. Your skin is so golden and glowy. No need for bronzer!"

"Yup. No bronzer for me," I agree lightheartedly. I want to feel that way. I do. I want to enjoy these moments with Livvie. But all I can think of is that she could have been the one in this seat...the one on the auction block...

She suddenly spins me on the stool. "No more looking until I'm done."

Minutes pass filled with more makeup, a curling iron, hairspray. So much hairspray. Then she's holding out my dress and nudging me to change. I slip into it and she does up the back zipper. It's simple, with a crisscross of fabric over the breasts and a ruched detail on one side of the waist. The hem falls just above my knee, the skirt making a soft flare over my hips.

It's not terrible, but it's certainly not the latest fashion. I really should have gone shopping in Italy before I came home.

Livvie shrugs and fusses over the dress, pulling, primping, adjusting.

"It's fine, Frankie. Put in your diamond studs and you'll spiffy it right up. Besides, who cares about the dress when you have a face like this? He won't be able to take his eyes off you."

Cupping my shoulders, she turns me to face the vanity. My brow lifts because surely, this isn't me in the reflection? A slow smile tips up my lips. It's been so long since I've dressed up that I hardly recognize myself. The makeup adds a glamorous kiss to my features and my hair looks, well, stunning if I'm being honest. Soft, big curls bounce around my shoulders and fall down my back. The dress still screams "outdated," but Livvie is right. I add diamond studs to my ears and my diamond drop pendant, and it gives the outfit polish.

I do not look half bad.

"You look *beautiful*. Stop scrunching your face and contemplating whether you're good enough." Livvie squeezes me. "You're perfect."

I put my hand over hers and catch her eyes in the mirror. I'm reminded once again that this has to be me, that I'm glad to take on the burden of this engagement so she doesn't have to. Livvie moves to put her things away, talking in a rush about the wedding. I'm touched that she read my body language enough to know what was playing out in my head. She still knows what my face scrunch is all about, and that means the world to me.

"Thank you, Liv."

My phone chirps with an alert that my driver is waiting outside, so I kiss my sister on the cheek, tell her I love her, and head downstairs. I let out a slow breath but it does nothing to steady my nerves. Walking to the front door feels like the path to my doom.

There's no turning back.

Outside, it's sunny and bright, instead of the overcast I was half expecting. Everything is golden and brilliant as I slip into the waiting car and sit stiffly on the drive to Bellanti Vineyards.

It's strange. Only two days ago, I had a sense of who I was. The person I'd worked so hard to bloom into while I was in Italy. I'd gotten on my plane back home with a fresh outlook on being a businesswoman, a winemaker, a daughter with a family business. Confidence, knowledge, physical strength. I'd amassed each of those things.

I feel none of them at the moment. I feel...hollow.

Squaring my shoulders, I sit up straighter, determined not to let this break me. It was my crazy idea to show up to meet my fiancé, unannounced, and I'm going to go through with it wearing a smile. It's either that or cry, and Livvie worked too hard on my makeup for that.

Movement outside my window pulls me from my thoughts. My throat goes tight as we pass through the elaborate iron gates of Bellanti Vineyards. The place is buzzing with tourists.

A man and woman ride past the car on horseback. I glance at them through the back window as we pull into the property and slowly roll down the drive. People mill around, holding glasses and chatting. Strategically placed café tables sit beneath pergolas heavy with masses of purple clematis. A tram runs along a track through the vineyard for tours, and I can see more guests on horseback riding along the hilltops. What I wouldn't give to be ten years old again, galloping on my pony through the vines, carefree as a lark.

The driveway curves gently, revealing a stately, imposing brownstone building. The windows are trimmed in black cast iron which match the gate and the hinges on the large arched front door. A Bellanti Main Offices sign hangs above the door. This is the heart of their empire.

"Here, please," I say to the driver. He parks and nods when I ask him to wait.

My insides pull with a thread of longing. This place is everything my family business used to be, and more. Now that I'm thinking about it, we have a stable on our property that's capable of housing enough horses to offer riding tours. And I'd already planned to create a few intimate seating areas and expand the menu, offering lunch options and picnic baskets to-go instead of just a few appetizers. Honestly, I was filled with so many ideas in Italy that being here is like a kick in the gut. The Bellantis have already pulled off everything I had in mind.

Sweet, warm air greets me as I slip out of the car and take the short walk into the belly of the beast. My shoes clip along smooth, polished slabs of stone. A receptionist's desk sits to the right, a prim young woman in a tight black skirt suit sitting behind it like it's her sworn duty to watch over every inch of this place. She cocks her head, giving me a pointed look as I approach with my shoulders thrown back and my chin held high.

"The tour offices are on the other side of the building," she tells me, eyeing my outfit.

"Actually, I'm here to see Dante Bellanti. Where might I find him?"

The woman tilts her head the other way. Up close, I realize how pretty she is, and how much younger than her heavy makeup and outfit first suggested. "Is he expecting you?"

"Yes. Well, not exactly. But...maybe if you let him know I'm here, he'll take a moment to see me."

She smiles tightly. "And you are?"

It's my turn to cock my head. I'm already tired of being judged. "His fiancée."

I've never seen such a perfect pair of stamped-on eyebrows arch so quickly. "I see. Please take a seat, and I'll let him know you're here."

A trio of plush leather chairs are artfully arranged around a free-standing electric fireplace on the wall behind me. I sit closest to the windows where I can see the activity outside. The sun streams in, golden rays offering warmth that would be comforting were the circumstances different. Instead I find myself sitting stiff, tight. It's the only way I can keep my nerves under control.

My shoulders start to ache a few minutes later, but I don't dare let my guard down. People in business attire come and go, their interactions fast and efficient.

Someone mentions Dante. She gives a quick nod and flicks a gaze at me, but looks away when I return the look.

Forty-five minutes later, I'm no longer nervous. I'm fuming.

The deep timbre of a male voice sounds from down the hallway past the receptionist's desk, followed by a different voice that calls out, "Sure thing. Thanks a lot, Dante."

I let out a breath. Dante's here. And he's kept me waiting almost an hour. Either he was on the world's longest phone call, or he just didn't care enough to see me. Enough.

I stand, smooth my dress, and plaster on a smile as I go back to the desk. Channeling Livvie, I muster up as much disarming sweetness as I can when I say, "Excuse me. I hate to be a bother, but is there a restroom? I didn't realize I'd be waiting so long."

The receptionist pauses, giving me a blasé look. I actually think she might deny me. I bat my eyelashes and widen my smile.

"Of course. It's that way. Back and to the left." She points down the hall.

"Thank you so much."

I wonder how far I can get before she can no longer see me. The hall splits into two corridors, the restroom on the left. Breezing past it, I continue along, discreetly reading the name plate beside each door until I finally reach an ornate carved door at the very end of the hall. It's unmarked, but it practically screams "In here."

A thread of the same deep voice I heard before filters through the door. Bingo.

I toss back my hair, take a breath, and turn the brass handle. The door swings open wide, and the conversation halts. Barging in, my breath catches in my throat as I get my first look at the man standing behind the desk. My fiancé's head swivels toward me, dark eyes immediately sizing me up as if evaluating a potential threat—which, let's face it, is probably exactly what he's doing. His chiseled face is strikingly handsome, something I wasn't expecting.

The angry words I'd been ready to toss at him stick in my throat. It's then that I notice an attractive redhead sitting behind the desk. She's leaning over a tablet with a stylus in her hand, showing off some deep cleavage. Dante's hand is on her arm, fingers splayed over her tanned flesh as if he'd been stroking her while she was taking notes.

Frozen in place, my eyes shift between Dante and this...woman. I'm struck by both how undeniably hot he is and how infuriated I am that he's flirting with someone else while he's engaged to me.

He comes around the desk, revealing an impressive body. "What is this?" His tone and body language tell me he's clearly annoyed at being interrupted.

Clearing my throat, I say, "I'm Frankie. Abbott. I just wanted to introduce myself—"

"Talk to Jessica," Dante interrupts. Then he rudely brushes past me and out the door, as if I'm completely insignificant.

Just like that, he's gone, leaving me with the redheaded woman.

"I...I just wanted to meet him," I say softly.

Jessica crosses her arms. "Mr. Bellanti is a busy man. He hates being interrupted at work, and you shouldn't be showing up here unexpectedly."

Charlie's words about staying out of her husband's business echo in my mind.

Standing, smoothing down the front of her tight red dress, the woman goes on, "Look, why don't you go home and take the next few hours to get ready for your scheduled dinner tonight? Maybe change into something a little more...current." She makes a circular gesture around my body, smirking. "Mr. Bellanti prefers his women in clothes from this century."

I dislike her. Like, a lot. I also have no retort.

As I watch her stroke her hand down the same arm that Dante had been touching, I suddenly know with a fierce certainty that she and my fiancé are fucking.

She walks over to me, and damn near pushes me toward the door.

"I'm leaving," I say.

"Good." Gripping my elbow, she guides me over the threshold. "Goodbye, now."

With that, she closes the door in my face, solidifying my suspicion that she's sleeping with Dante.

For some reason, that makes me angrier than anything.

4

FRANKIE

When I was a kid, I used to stand in front of the open refrigerator after school, convinced that if I stared hard enough, something delicious would magically appear.

That wishful thinking didn't work then, and it's no more effective now as I gaze into my dated closet, glaring into the expanse of crappy clothes. I literally have nothing appropriate to wear to my dinner with Dante tonight, and thanks to Jessica's bitchy comments, I'm even more worried about it than I was before.

Jessica.

I throw down the hanger in my hand and grab a handful of other outfits. No. No, no, and no. I toss them all onto the ever-growing reject pile, my emotions still swinging violently between rage and desperation. My fiancé isn't just an asshole, he's a philandering asshole. And to make matters worse? He's doing it with an employee. Someone I'll probably have to see more than I'd like, considering I'm marrying into the family business. Though why I ever thought he'd be loyal to me is anybody's guess.

Still, it's not the kind of relationship I want for myself. I know I deserve better. I deserve love and kindness and gentleness and real connection. The kind of relationship where we can curl up on the couch and talk about our day, or laugh over stupid television commercials, or just sit in comfortable silence and appreciate each other.

Longing stirs in me with a familiar pang. My eyes burn, and I realize I have to put away any possibility of experiencing true love or fidelity in this marriage. Those are childish wishes, the dreams of a teenager with a crush and hopes for a rosy-pink future.

The kind of dreams that only get people into trouble anyway.

My cell vibrates on my vanity. I answer Charlie's call and put my phone on speaker.

"Tell me everything," she chirps. "I want all the juicy details about your meeting with Dante. Wait, but first tell me the plan for the winery. What are they thinking for expansion, or wait, are they even keeping our winery as a winery or are they going to—oh no, they're not going to shut it down, are they? Where am I going to run my business, then? Will we still have jobs? I can't stand all these unknowns! Why aren't you saying anything?"

I'm sure Charlie's been on pins and needles with the uncertainty. She's been operating an event planning business from our winery for the past two years and things have really taken off.

"Because there's nothing *to* say. We never got that far. He left before I even finished introducing myself."

"What? You're kidding."

"I wish I was." I relay the events, cringing as I relive the abject failure and embarrassment of those sparse minutes in Dante's office. "Also I think he's screwing his assistant. I mean, it's pretty obvious."

"Oh my God." Charlie takes a pointed breath. "Look, sis, the only way you have a chance in hell of surviving this marriage is to set some ground rules."

"Ground rules? He wouldn't give me the time of day. I barely said my name before he stormed out, and that woman—who was definitely not in appropriate office attire, might I add—basically *tossed me out!*"

She huffs and I imagine her flopping onto her sofa with a hand over her eyes, the way she does when she's stressed. If I can't manage a short introductory meeting with my own fiancé, how am I going to be able to set any rules?

"Look, Char. Dante doesn't really want me. He's not interested. He's just after the business and for some crazy reason, maybe just to make an example of Dad, he decided he'd take a wife to go with it. Point is, I'm insignificant in this transaction. I promise I'll do everything I can to protect our family, and our jobs, but...it's pretty unlikely I'll be able to negotiate with him."

She huffs again, this time sounding personally insulted. "You can't just let this jerk walk all over you. Are you going to be the doormat, Frankie? Just lie there and let him and his slut wipe their shoes all over you? I don't think so. You're an Abbott, and we do not lie down for anybody."

I sink onto my bed and rub my eyes. "Fine, then what do you expect me to do?"

"Grow a pair!" she barks through the speakerphone. "Go back over there and figure this out. Make him listen to you. Make him take your damn hand for a proper shake while you say, 'Hello, Dante. I'm Francesca. Your soon-to-be wife.' If you let him act like this now, you'll never have a leg to stand on later."

She's right. She's so right. But going back to the Bellanti winery and facing Humiliation, Round Two is more than I want to take on right now. I still feel sick from Round One.

"I have dinner with him in a few hours. That will give me time to prepare. And, you know, work on my courage."

"Okay, good. I know you're probably still shell-shocked by all this. It was a shock to everyone." Her voice trails off and then she picks her way into the next sentence. "So, uh...have you talked to Rico since you got home?"

It's my turn to let loose a dramatic huff. The urge to hang up the phone nearly overtakes me, but I don't. Instead I flop back onto the bed with a groan.

"No, I haven't spoken to Rico, nor will I, so drop it."

"But—"

A pang of longing goes through me. "I said drop it, Charlie."

"Okay, okay. Dropping it."

Clearing my throat, I get up and rummage through my closet again. It's hopeless. Nothing spectacular magically appeared while I wasn't looking. Dammit.

"I hear hangers clicking. Are you digging through your closet?"

"Yes."

"Did you make a huge pile on the floor that you're contemplating setting on fire?"

"Y...es."

She snickers and it pulls a laugh out of me. "It's hopeless, Charlie. I've got nothing."

"Nonsense. Just pull out your most alluring dress and wear that."

There's a stretch of silence in which I wait for her to realize what she just said, and what my reply is going to be. She knows as well as I do that I never cared much for clothes, and that my wardrobe hasn't miraculously updated itself while I've been in Tuscany. She's the sister with the latest designer everything. She's always been way more fashion focused than me and Liv.

"You're going to say you don't have anything alluring, aren't you?" she says with a sigh.

"Yep. Which especially sucks after Mr. Bellanti's assistant specified that he prefers his women in clothes *from this century.*"

Charlie gasps. "Bitch!"

"Bitch," I agree.

"Hmm." The sound of hangers clacking together through the phone makes me grin. Charlie is in her closet, rummaging through her boutique-quality

39

wardrobe. She makes sounds of contemplation as she rifles through. "I have a lot here. You have time to run over real quick?"

"My boobs are way bigger than yours," I point out. "And you're taller with a slimmer waist and hips. I doubt you have anything that will work for me."

"Oh, screw your tig old biddies! I've got the perfect thing. I'll have a courier bring it right over."

I know from experience that nothing my sister owns will fit me right, but I'm not about to argue with her. "Okay, if you think it will fit."

"It will fit. Call me as soon as you leave the dinner tonight. I won't be able to sleep until I know how it goes! Oh, and send me a pic of you in the dress. Gotta run. Love you!"

She clicks off. I stare at the mute phone for a moment before returning to my pile of useless clothes. After cleaning up the mess, I assess myself in the bathroom mirror.

My makeup still looks decent, but it could use a touch-up before dinner. I could beg Livvie to help me again, but soon she and Charlie won't be here to glam me up every time I need it. If this marriage agreement requires that I make a lot of appearances with my husband, I'm going to need to step up my primp game. The Bellantis seem to always have their hands in something. They're at every event, every party. Every wedding and business grand opening. Every winery seasonal opener.

I never imagined myself in this kind of life. I always

thought I'd run the family winery behind the scenes, not be at the forefront of it. That was supposed to be Charlie's job, and Livvie too, with her bubbly personality. Eventually.

To think that she could be in my place right now, getting ready for dinner with a Bellanti. Sold as part of a business deal. I can only imagine what all this would do to her tender spirit, her warm, loving heart. No, a man like Dante Bellanti doesn't deserve someone like Livvie.

Charlie is right. I need to grow a pair, maybe two, and set some rules with my fiancé. I don't want to be a doormat any more than I want to be his wife, but at least I can have some say in how our marriage operates.

The sound of the doorbell sends me rushing down the stairs. The courier is at the door, just as Charlie promised, holding out a white garment bag with a designer's name stamped on it in gold foil. I'm a little too curious to see what's inside—excited, even. Though I wish I were dressing for a different occasion. Something to actually be excited about.

Back in my room, I set the bag on the bed and unzip it. The dress still has the tags on it—it's clearly brand new, and just purchased in my size.

It's a beautifully rich purple, the exact shade to bring out the violet undertones in my blue eyes. I stroke the silk charmeuse, which feels ridiculously expensive. Slipping into it in front of my mirror, a little shiver goes through me. The dress clings like a second skin while still managing to keep me completely covered from neck to mid-calf. The neckline hugs the base of my throat, there's artful draping over the bust, and the fitted waist gives me a slim line. Long sleeves slightly flutter at the wrist, making me feel demure yet sexy. It's the perfect combination of date night and business.

I have to admit, it shows off my figure perfectly without giving too much away. This isn't an occasion that I'm excited about by any means, and I hate that I have to do this.

But thank goodness for sisters who make me look hot while I do.

5

FRANKIE

My father has officially ruined us.

It's apparent judging by the looks I get as I step into the new restaurant on the edge of Napa, Bella Notte. Despite the fact that the place just opened recently, I spot half a dozen family acquaintances at the tables in the dining area—which is only to be expected when you live in a small town. Their eyes drill into me as I approach the hostess stand.

I give a little wave to a woman and her partner, both looking straight at me. They snub my greeting and turn back to their meals. Another couple stares at me in distaste, but most of the familiar faces are turned away now, blatantly ignoring me.

An older woman hazards a brief smile, and I smile back, but it seems that whatever my father did to ruin our family name was unforgivable. People aren't quick to let go of grudges around here, especially where their wine is concerned.

What will people say when they find out I'm engaged to Dante Bellanti?

Damn my father to hell.

The hostess takes my name and shows me to a secluded private table in the back. It's empty. I sit and immediately notice there are place settings for three.

"Has Mr. Bellanti arrived yet?" I ask.

"No, ma'am. Would you care for a glass of house red while you're waiting?"

Of course Dante is running late to a dinner he set up. Men like him are always making power plays. Or maybe this is my punishment for showing up uninvited to the Bellanti offices today. I wonder how long he's going to keep me waiting.

"The house red sounds perfect," I say. "Thank you."

God knows I need something to calm my nerves.

I glance around and take in the beautiful ambiance. Large wood beams, stained dark, span across the white stucco ceiling. Soft lights glow from modern iron fixtures overhead, while soothing jazz music plays in the background. If the substance of this meeting were different, I might actually be able to enjoy myself.

My wine arrives. The time ticks on and I've downed half of it and still no Bellanti. I've got my flaws, but being late isn't one of them—and honestly, this isn't a good look on a man of his supposed power. Is it a personality flaw, or is he doing it on purpose?

"Ah, you're here."

My attention is pulled to the deep voice with an

unmistakable bored tone. Dante approaches with the barest look at me, the complete opposite of my reaction.

I can't look away.

His suit fits him like it's been hand molded to his tall, fit body. His hair is perfectly combed back with a touch of sexy waves that look hard to contain. The forest green stripes on his tie compliment his coloring and accentuates the lines of his masculine throat. Jesus.

Focus, Frankie. I'm here to grow a pair and negotiate, yet my eyes wander lower, lower, wondering about *his* pair...

"Drinking alone? Looks like you've almost finished your wine."

The female voice coming from behind him takes me by surprise.

Jessica. Shit.

She sidles up to Dante with a brilliant smile on perfect red, glossy lips. She's draped in an emerald, off-the-shoulder dress that makes her red hair pop and her cleavage, well, it's out there for the world to see. There isn't a thread on this woman out of place and I suddenly feel very second class in the dress I'd loved only moments ago.

I don't respond to her taunt.

Dante pulls a seat out for Jessica to his left, then sits between me and her. My skin tingles at his proximity, the feeling going lower as I catch the woodsy-citrus scent of his cologne.

"Jessica is here to take notes on this meeting, of

course." Dante juts a finger into the air and a waiter immediately appears with a tray of drinks.

I nod in agreement, even manage to give Jessica a warm smile as if it doesn't bother me a bit that she's here. She licks her lips, puckering them a little as Dante glances at her before taking a slow sip of her wine. Her gaze darts back to me, probably to see if I noticed her seductive little gesture.

"Let's get started, shall we?" Dante says.

He flips open a leather folder. Papers on official Bellanti Vineyards letterhead are tucked neatly inside, as well as some legal documents. He thumbs through them and withdraws three copies of a single page, handing one to me and another to Jessica. It's a list of apparent topics we need to discuss.

I barely have time to scan it—wifely responsibilities, household duties, expectation of heirs—when Jessica clears her throat and slides on a slim pair of reading glasses. She tilts her head studiously, putting on her best sexy librarian show.

"Item one," she reads aloud. "Wedding details."

"Wedding details?" I repeat softly. An actual nuptial ceremony hadn't really crossed my mind; I'd assumed we'd simply sign papers at the courthouse and be done with it.

"It's ten days from now." Dante's voice is tinged in annoyance, as if he's explaining the obvious to someone not quite able to comprehend.

I look squarely at him, the force of it drawing his attention. Our eyes meet and I damn near lose my breath. "Right. We're getting married in ten days and we still haven't had proper introductions." I thrust out a hand. "Francesca Abbott. So very nice to officially meet you."

He hesitates before sliding his palm against mine and wrapping his strong fingers around my knuckles with a little more grip than is probably necessary. One side of his mouth turns up, but only for a fraction of a second before his tempting lips resume a neutral line across his face.

"Dante Bellanti, but presumably you already knew that."

I nod. "Very nice to meet you, Mr. Bellanti."

There goes his lip again. Huh. So he likes being called Mr. Bellanti. I make a mental note to never refer to him that way again.

Jessica clears her throat again and taps her pen against her list. "The ceremony will take place at Bellanti Vineyards. Intimate, but lavish. The guest list is small. Your immediate family has been invited, of course. Please provide me with a list of any additional guests you'd like to invite by end of day tomorrow. Do you have any requests for decor, music, food?"

"I'm happy to leave the styling to the wedding planner. Although," I add sweetly, "it's a real shame we don't have a special song for our first dance, isn't it? But I've got a couple of suggestions. How about, 'What's Love Got to Do with It?' by Tina Turner. Or..."

"'You Give Love a Bad Name,' perhaps," Dante suggests.

His quip robs the words from my mouth. I narrow my eyes and regroup. "'Love is a Battlefield.'"

The smile he's been trying so hard to fight blossoms now, just enough to transform his expression from stone cold to slightly evil with a side of hella-sexy. "Yes, Ms. Abbott, if you're not careful it certainly can be."

Jessica interrupts. "We can revisit this topic. In fact, let's just scratch it all together. Next item, catering."

Dante waves a dismissive hand. "Nonnegotiable. The menu has already been decided. The order is in."

"Fine with me," I say coolly.

"Okay," Jessica says, checking it off. "Expectations of wifely duties pertaining to—"

"Also nonnegotiable." He spears me with a look. "You're expected to act as any wife would. Attend events by my side, host parties, decorate, plan menus, and whatever else women in this position do."

I draw back. "I...don't decorate. Or cook. If you're expecting me to throw lavish parties and refresh the interior decor, I'm going to need to hire that out."

Jessica huffs a quiet, stunted laugh. "If you're really that inept, I'm sure we can arrange a stipend."

"I wasn't raised to be arm candy, sadly," I shoot back. "I was raised to know what kinds of fertilizer help virgin vines get their best start, what time of day is ideal for harvesting grapes, how to choose the opacity of wine bottles to cure the best vintage. None of that came with cooking lessons, I'm afraid."

Dante makes a sound and looks to his hands.

Jessica purses her lips. "Living arrangements?"

"It's night time, by the way," I say. "The heat of the day alters the acidity and sugar composition of the grapes. As for living arrangements, I prefer to keep my residence at my—"

"You'll reside at Bellanti House, with me," Dante interrupts.

I don't like that one bit. Attempting to assert myself, I say, "Well, maybe I can split my time between there and my father's house—"

"Absolutely not," my fiancé says.

This is pointless. Dante and Jessica are overriding my every thought. But that doesn't mean I'm going down without a fight. I can still lay down some boundaries.

I tilt my head. "Fine, then I want my own rooms."

"Perfect! No sharing a bed," Jessica agrees flippantly, jotting it on her paper. Dante and I both look at her. Her eyebrows jet up, her porcelain cheeks growing pink.

Dante says, "Thank you, Jessica. That will be all for this evening. You may go."

She smiles, not budging. "Why don't I just write down which rooms you'd prefer Francesca to take? That way I can be sure the decorators…"

Her voice trails off as Dante levels her with a stare. Her attempts to backpedal have clearly failed.

Seeing Dante's narrowed eyes, my stomach drops— and the look wasn't even meant for me. Jessica's throat moves quickly as she swallows hard, puts on a tight smile, and gathers her things. With a nod, she scurries for the door, just as the waiter appears with a tray of appetizers.

"We didn't order yet—" I start to say, but Dante waves away my comment.

"I took care of it."

The food smells delicious, but my insides are so twisted up, I'm not sure I can partake of any of it. "Of course you did."

The waiter refills our wineglasses and leaves us. Dante turns to me. It's the most he's been fully attuned to me since he got here. His dark eyes on me. His powerful body angled toward me. His attention, one-hundred percent on me. I'm afraid and turned on at the same time.

"Now, then." His voice is seductively low and edged with gravel. "I expect an heir. We will have children, thus we will be sharing a bed."

A pang hits me between the legs and I have the sudden urge to squeeze my thighs together. He hasn't come close to touching me, yet my mind wants to prance around with sudden dirty thoughts of this man putting a baby in me. Ridiculous.

"You have brothers," I point out. "They can provide an heir. I see no need for us to have anything beyond a marriage of convenience."

"The Bellanti name will live on through *my* line."

I take a generous sip of my wine and then challenge him with, "I was never consulted on whether or not I wanted children."

He leans forward. A deep, shocking warmth spreads over my thigh, and I realize he's put his hand there. His fingers tighten and the needy pulse between my legs goes haywire. All of a sudden, he's all I can focus on, my insides gone taut as a wire.

"You're to be my wife," he says. "Wives give their husbands children. Your opinion on the matter is neither required nor welcome. I *will* have sons."

He slides his hand up higher, sliding the silk of my skirt with it. The fabric flutters and bunches over my bare skin, creating a rush of sensation as he kneads my inner thigh.

"Fine," I say. "But you can't sleep with anyone else."

Little lines gather at the outer corners of his eyes, marking his sarcastic smile before his lips do. "Don't be a child." His hands moves higher again, and I find myself holding my breath as his fingertips almost reach my underwear. "I'll be discreet. No one will know."

Anger begins pushing the lust aside. My fingers curl into my palms as I war with my body. "Then no sex until I'm fertile. There's no need to engage in intimacy unless it's time for impregnation."

I lift my chin and glare at him, the fire in his eyes scorching me. But I don't look away.

"You don't have a leg to stand on, Francesca. You can't negotiate with me. I own your winery and I own *you*. Whether I wanted you or not, you're mine and *you'll do as I say*."

My breath comes hard and fast. I'm shaking as my fury builds and builds. Suddenly his fingers feel like a predator's claws and I want to slap his hand away. How could I have been turned on by a man like this? He never wanted me at all. Was it my baby sister he craved?

I'm a few years younger than Dante, but Livvie...she's practically still a girl. The thought that he may have had his eye on her all along disgusts me.

Slowly, he moves back, taking his hand with him. Without another word, he chooses a foie gras toast from the appetizer tray and sets it in front of me.

"Eat," he commands. "By the way, I appreciate this dress on you. It brings out the color of your eyes."

He smiles, and I silently vow to never wear the damn thing again.

In fact, maybe I'll burn it when I get home.

6

FRANKIE

This definitely isn't what I imagined my wedding day looking like when I was ten years old.

A week and a half later, I'm standing in front of a mirror looking at myself in a dress I didn't choose, getting ready to marry a stranger. I'm the picture of a perfect bride in a stunning, elaborate lace gown with long sleeves and a neckline that plunges to my sternum. A sheer veil hangs down over my curls and a tiny, sparkly tiara holds it in place. I look like I should be on the cover of a bridal magazine.

I look nothing like myself.

This dress? It's clearly made to be photographed in, and not much else. The skirt is so tight around my thighs that I doubt I'll be able to manage much more than penguin walk, and I can't imagine actually dancing with this ridiculous mermaid train trailing behind me.

When I was a girl, I always dreamed of a gown in a softer ivory shade, with a simple V-neck and spaghetti straps, embroidery climbing up the full skirt. Something I could twirl and dance in, but also be comfortable wearing.

Of course, I also wanted the groom to ride up on a white horse, sweep me into his arms, and lead us off into the sunset at a full gallop. The only thing I'm getting swept up in now is my own personal hell, hitched to the son of a mob boss, stripped of my family business and my autonomy. You know, the things every little girl dreams of.

The morning after my dinner with Dante, Jessica sent over an itinerary and summary of the wedding details, including the seating chart, catering menu, and images of the wedding and bridesmaids' dresses. A tailor showed up soon after to get my measurements, and my dress arrived at the crack of dawn this morning by courier.

It's dumbfounding how my entire wedding was planned without any input from me. Apparently, the invitations had been sent as soon as my father made the deal with Dante. How was it possible that I was the last one to know? Well, me and my sisters, I suppose. If they'd received their invitations weeks ago like everyone else, they would have called me right away.

Jessica, I'm assuming, had been in charge of all the logistics. I can't quite shake the bad taste in my mouth over the fact that she orchestrated this whole thing.

Letting out a breath, I turn this way and that before the oval mirror and assess the dress yet again. Despite the fact that it isn't my style, the tailor really did an amazing job fitting the bodice to me like a glove. The fine, hand-made lace hugs my shoulders and breasts, the white satin beneath glimmering slightly in the light. As much as I hate to admit it, it's beautiful. Not something I would have ever chosen for myself, but flattering, showing off my curves with an elegant silhouette. I bet Jessica picked it out. My fiancé's mistress does have great taste. And nope, I'm not bitter about that at all. Not one tiny bit. I just love that that bitch chose my dress.

The doors suddenly burst open and my sisters come in, interrupting my brooding. Livvie squeals and claps her hands together as she comes up behind me.

"Frankie! Oh my goodness! You're a vision."

I roll my eyes. "You literally zipped up my dress, Liv. You've already seen me."

"I know, I know. I'm just so excited and happy for you!" She bounces a little, her heels clicking on the marble floor, and I can't help smiling at her youthful enthusiasm.

I turn and look at my sisters, both of them startlingly gorgeous in pale blue, halter-style bridesmaid dresses. It's a hue that equally complements Liv's cornsilk blonde hair and Charlie's deep golden shade, playing up their blue eyes, too.

"You two look like literal angels," I say.

"Of course we do! It's your fairy-tale wedding, Frankie." Livvie clasps her hands together. "Just wait until you see what they've done outside."

Charlie nods, her mood more subdued than Liv's. "The decor is stunning. So classy."

"I'm sure it is." I take Livvie's hand and give it a squeeze. "I can't wait to see it."

The lie is sour on my tongue. I'd prefer to never see it; to run as far and fast from this nightmare as I can. Livvie starts primping my dress, nitpicking over this and that.

"It's just so dreamy. Your groom looks like a model, I swear! You could have done worse, Frankie, that's for sure. He's left no detail out. Just wait, you'll see. This dress is fantastic. Italian lace and French silk."

Normally I enjoy my youngest sister's banter, but right now, every word is rubbing me wrong. I don't care how good Dante looks, or about the details. Each second that ticks by brings me closer to becoming someone I don't want to be.

I don't want to be a Bellanti and I sure as hell don't want to be Dante Bellanti's wife.

My chest swells with a stifling breath. Suddenly my dress is too tight and my lungs can't fill. I'm trapped inside lace and silk. I feel like I'm going to pass out. Oh, God.

The swish of Charlie's dress is loud in my ears as she hurries over to me and puts her hands on my shoulders, steadying me.

"All right, Livvie," she says over her shoulder. "Time for you to scoot. I need to have a quick chat with Frankie...*alone.*"

Livvie steps back and looks between us, a sly smile pulling her lips. "Okay, okay, I get it." She nods knowingly, then gives me an amused look. "I figured you'd know all about sexing up a man by now, sis, but you do you."

She winks and saunters out the door.

Charlie bursts out laughing as soon as the door closes. "She thinks I'm going to have the sex talk with you."

"You're not, though, right? Because I'm good."

Charlie takes my hand and threads her fingers through mine. The touch grounds me as little flames of panic dance inside me.

"Just take a breath, Frankie. In and out. There you go...in and out."

Tears sting my eyes. "He's awful. How am I supposed to actually go through with this?" My voice cracks and I turn away with a wave of my hand.

"No, no, no. You'll ruin your makeup. Frankie, just *breeeeathe*."

Charlie grabs a box of tissues and puts one in my hand before pulling me to the sofa and guiding me to sit. Somehow, I manage to force down my tears, but the panic is slower to give up. Sinking down beside me, Charlie takes my hand again.

"Listen. I'm going to explain the rules of being a wife to a man with mafia ties."

Mafia wife. Me. Oh my God.

Swallowing hard, I look at our hands and nod. Attempting to speak will just force the sobs out, and once I break down, I know I won't be able to pull myself back together.

"The main thing to remember is that all Dante expects from you is to look pretty on his arm and warm his bed. Aside from those two things, your interactions with him will be limited. Trust me when I say he won't want you involved in any other aspects of his life. I know that sounds harsh, and it is, a little bit. But that's the reality of what you're getting into. Sex. Look pretty. Keep quiet. Raise the kids, if and when. That's it."

She's doing a shit job of making me feel better. "How is that any kind of life?" I ask.

"Your life is still your own. Even if he has rules and demands, it's not like he's going to be home breathing down your neck all the time. You still get to do you, you just have to be clever about it. Keep it low key. Okay?"

I nod. Maybe she has a point. What Dante doesn't know won't hurt him.

Charlie goes on, "Never ask about his business, what he's doing, or where he's been. Don't stick your nose into anything. Let him take care of shit. And if he says he's going to handle a problem, just trust that he will and don't ask how. Never, ever ask how."

"Jesus, Char." The words croak out of me.

She squeezes my hand. "It's very easy to fool men into thinking women are simple creatures. Like I said, he'll be happy to leave you alone if you just follow the rules."

"I get it," I say, tracing the pattern of the lace on my skirt. The panic is gone. Now I'm just depressed. "You're telling me to play dumb and be compliant so I can live a relatively peaceful life. A life where I *might* be able to do the things I want, as long as I give my husband lots of sex, keep my mouth shut, and look pretty. I am *so excited* to say I do right now."

Charlie sighs. "Hey. You're saving Livvie. You know that, right?" She leans over and presses her forehead to mine. "You're not committing yourself to the Bellantis, you're committing yourself to saving this family. To keeping it safe. We're the last of the Abbotts. We gotta stick together."

The change of tactics hits me in the gut, and I can't sit still any longer. Standing, I smooth my skirt and return to the mirror. The image in the glass is a lie: I look calm, poised, flawless. I never considered myself much of an actress, but maybe I can pull this off after all.

A knock on the door makes my heart leap into my throat. Oh God, it can't possibly be time yet, can it? I'm not ready!

"Just a minute!" I call out.

The door opens. My eyes track the movement as if I'm watching a movie in slow motion. Not ready, not ready, not—

"Francesca, oh, how lovely."

A middle-aged woman in a stylish navy dress strides in. She's wearing an outrageous hat with tulle and pheasant feathers spraying from the top and a brim wide enough to cover her face. She quietly closes the door and lifts her head, deep magenta lipstick making her smile glow.

Charlie and I glance at each other before looking back at her, our voices equal in timing and exasperation.

"Hello, Mom."

7

FRANKIE

HONESTLY, I'd forgotten all about my mother—because I figured she'd never show. Yet here she is, dressed like she's headed to the Kentucky Derby instead of her daughter's wedding.

She gives Charlie a sweet look which we both know is laced with poison.

"I'd like to speak with my daughter on her wedding day, if you don't mind. Alone?"

Charlie doesn't budge and for a split second, I'm glad. Knowing our mother, she won't back down until she gets her way, and I don't need a scene before my nuptials. Still, I give my sister a nod of reassurance, and after a long look at our mom, she leaves.

Mom sighs happily and takes a seat in a plush chair next to the mirror, angled just enough that she can catch her reflection. She holds her hands out to me, her gaze so intense that I nearly squirm. But then I remember who she really is and the discomfort is replaced by stubborn indifference.

"Come, now." She motions with her fingers that I step forward and take her hands. Reluctantly, I do. The feel of her hands squeezing mine fills me with distaste. "You look very beautiful today, Francesca."

Besides strangers or new acquaintances, only my mother calls me that to my face. Using my full name when she knows I prefer Frankie is just one more way for her to willfully misunderstand me. To make a point out of having things done *her* way—as always.

"I remember being where you are," she croons. "You don't have to do this, you know."

I pull free of her grip, Livvie's face flashing in my mind. "Yes, I do."

"Francesca—"

No, she's not going to do this to me. Not today and not anytime soon. It took me a long time and a lot of energy to work through the wounds she caused. The last thing I need before I walk down the aisle is the pain of them all over again, fresh and smarting.

"You don't know me, Mom," I tell her. "You have no idea what's going on or what my life is like, because you decided not to be a part of it when you left. So why don't you go sit down and enjoy the free wine?"

Hurt flickers across her face. I don't believe it, but it's there. She whisks it away with another smile but not fast enough. Why does it make me satisfied that I hurt her for once? Jesus, I don't need this right now.

She stands with a small sniffle—to make me feel guilty, probably.

"You really do look beautiful, darling."

She pauses for my response but I don't give her one, and she leaves. The door clicks shut, closing the rest of the world out so I can sink onto the settee in front of the mirror and gather myself. Who cares what I look like? What good is it to be beautiful when you're being forced to marry a criminal, a controlling asshole who's screwing his assistant.

My mind takes off with all the things wrong with this marriage and every dark scenario I'm about to step into. Tearing my gaze away from the mirror, I jerk at another knock on the door. It opens and my father strides in easily. His demeanor is casual, as if this is just another day and he had no part in selling me off to the mob.

"It's time," he says, sliding his hands into his trouser pockets. There's an almost gleeful twinkle in his blue eyes, a light that I haven't seen before. He's...happy about this.

Giddy, even.

Searching his face, all I can muster in return is a glare. He sold us out, all of us. Our winery is gone, our legacy wiped. And now he's standing here smiling from ear to ear, like he can hardly wait to lead me down the aisle to fulfill his dirty promise.

I rise and try to walk past him, but he snags my arm as I cross the threshold and pulls me back with a pointed look. Then he wraps my hand around his forearm and leads me down the hallway, around the corner where the golden hue of the sun reaches inside.

Arched barn doors are open, leading us into the winery courtyard, where my heels click on the cobblestone as we enter the mouth of the vineyard. As expected, Bellanti Vineyards are turned out in full show mode. Sprays of expensive-looking flowers adorn every flat surface, with more bouquets hanging from the trees. Elegant white chairs with sheer ribbons sit in perfect rows, holding even more perfectly dressed guests. All eyes are on me.

All of them.

More greenery is draped over the large pergola where my groom and the priest await me. Lights twinkle from the branches of live oaks and weeping pepper trees. My gorgeous sisters are lined up on one side of the pergola, Dante's brothers and friends (or business associates?) in their tuxes on the opposite side. Everything is impressively elegant and perfect and I didn't choose any of it, least of all the man waiting for me at the end of the aisle.

It's surreal. I feel like I'm fighting through a bad dream as my father leads me to my fate. A string quartet plays the wedding march, sounding tinny and small in my ears. I keep my eyes focused straight ahead at the dark outline of my groom, who doesn't even have the decency to watch me walk down the aisle. He's looking down, then to the side, then up as if assessing the weather. Anywhere but at me.

The music fades as I reach Dante. My father deposits me at my groom's side, drops my hand like it's on fire, and disappears. I guess we're not doing the whole "who gives this woman in marriage" part. Nor, obviously, the part where the groom acknowledges his bride before him, maybe even tearing up a little when he sees how pretty she looks.

Nope, because my future husband is a hell of a lot more interested in the platinum blonde sitting in the second row off to my left. I caught his gaze as it bounced over to her, and it's currently still stuck there.

"Family, friends. Welcome all, on this glorious day."

The priest's voice gets Dante's attention and he finally looks at me as he turns to face the priest. Nothing registers on his face, his expression inscrutable. Looking past him to his brothers who stand in the line of groomsmen beside him, I find Armani wearing the same somber expression as Dante. Marco, the youngest, grins at me and winks, and I turn away.

Dante's tuxedo is pure perfection and were this a different story altogether, I'd take the time to really appreciate how well it fits him. How stunning and honestly, panty-melting he looks in it. But this isn't a love story. It's duty.

No wonder he won't look at me. He feels the same, of course.

I zone out during the ceremony, doing everything I can to hold it together, until suddenly the priest is asking us to speak our vows. What a joke. I already know Dante isn't planning to honor his.

He and I turn toward each other. He takes my hands in his, loosely, without any of the power he exhibited during our handshake at dinner. It's as if he doesn't want to be touching me at all. Someone hands me a men's wedding band. Whatever the priest has said up to this point, I've blocked it out. Half the wedding already over and I have no recollection of it as I stand facing a man who's making it very clear that he doesn't want me.

"Francesca Abbott, do you promise to love, honor, and obey Dante as his wife, dutifully, faithfully, as long as you both shall live?"

I know I need to answer, but I don't want to. And then I remember my sisters. They're the ones I think of, and in lieu of my vows, I make a sincere, silent pledge to always keep them safe—especially Livvie, who looks so fresh and happy for me that I can hardly stand it.

"I-I do," I say.

The priest gives a subtle gesture, prompting me to slide the ring onto Dante's finger.

"Dante Bellanti, do you promise to love and honor Francesca, dutifully, faithfully, as long as you both shall live?"

No obeying for the groom, of course.

The corner of his mouth twitches. His eyes are hard as stone as he slides both the engagement ring and a slim wedding band on me—neither of which I've seen yet.

"I do," he says.

Liar. The word nearly pops out of my mouth. He has no intention of loving me. I glance over at my sisters again. Livvie is grinning from ear to ear. I'm doing this for her. For Charlie.

"I now pronounce you man and wife."

I snap back to my—oh my God, my husband—just as he reaches for my veil. Lifts it. His dark hair glints in the sunlight and something flickers in his eyes. A spark of interest, perhaps. My heart flips in anticipation as he leans in to kiss me, but my body is stiff and I don't fluidly lean in to meet him. It must show, because suddenly his hand is behind my head and he's pulling me toward him. Closer, closer until his hot breath touches my mouth and his lips are on mine, his tongue demanding to get between them as he forces me to open for him. I pull in a shocked breath through my nose, my cheeks flaming with heat as he punishes me with his kiss.

My lips tingle, little sparks of heat flicking over my skin as his tongue slides along mine, tasting me, demanding to know me. I'm woozy with the force of the kiss, my knees going watery. It's time to pull back...this has gone on too long for a public kiss... but he won't let go. My neck throbs from the force of my pulse there. The tingling grows, the sparks multiplying.

Finally, Dante slowly breaks away. I take a breath while his lips still touch mine, barely, just barely. His eyes bore into mine, and then he takes my lower lips between his teeth and presses the tender flesh. I jerk as the pressure promises pain, but he lets me go, putting space between us so quickly that I nearly falter.

There's a pause from our guests before someone in the back starts to clap, and then all of them do, followed by cheers and whistles and I swear that I've never been so embarrassed in my life. My legs quiver, my hands shake. Dante takes my arm and loops it through his with an amused sidelong glance. He looks at me again, and he must notice the heat in my flaming cheeks, because for the first time all day he smiles.

"Ah, there's my blushing bride."

Livvie coos with delight behind me, clapping furiously. She still believes I agreed to this marriage willingly, and I'm glad for it. Let her enjoy the day. At least one of us can.

The unfamiliar weight on my finger prompts me to look down at the rings situated there. The wedding band is eternity style, set all around with small sparkling diamonds; the engagement ring sports a huge, flawless, emerald cut diamond surrounded by sapphires. Funny to get my engagement ring during the wedding. I wonder if Jessica chose the rings, too?

There's a slight tug on my arm as Dante leads me out of the pavilion and down the aisle. I catch the eyes landing on me as I pass. Friends. Neighbors. Business acquaintances.

My mother.

She's frowning beneath the brim of her egregious hat and I can't tell if it's from displeasure or something else. Not that it matters.

I lift my chin as I walk by, straightening my spine. I won't falter in front of her, or anyone else. My mother might be a quitter, but I'm not.

I won't walk away from my responsibilities. I won't fail. I'll make the best of my life and whatever comes next.

Delores Alvarez is two rows down. Her eyes track me

as I approach. They're sad, worried. Her smile tight. My resolve wavers, because I actually care what she thinks. But I'll never show it. Never.

Steeling myself, I smile—no, I beam—as I glide past. It doesn't matter what happens the rest of the day, or what anyone thinks. I have to get through this.

I'm a Bellanti now, and come hell or high water, I'm determined to finish out my wedding as the picture of a perfect bride.

FRANKIE

THE RECEPTION IS HELD in a side courtyard created just for the occasion. The vineyard stretches out behind us in gradient shades of green that glimmer in the late afternoon sun. Everything is pure perfection. The tables are decorated with topiaries of greenery and golden edged geometric holders sporting flickering candles.

It's beautiful, of course.

Expensive blue and gold carpets act as runners over the ground and between the tables, while cast iron poles hold lanterns with fairy lights wrapped around their length. Waitstaff move easily through the guests, offering drinks and setting out trays of hors d'oeuvres. Dante leads me to the head table, but we're stopped every few seconds by well-wishers, most of whom I block out because my brain hasn't yet caught up with the reality of the situation.

The reality that this has actually happened.

My lips still feel bruised from the kiss and I'm not

sure the heated blush will ever fade from my cheeks. Dante guides me to my seat in the center of the table and brushes my hand off his arm as he moves away to speak to someone. Carefully arranging my skirt and train, I sink into my seat and reach for the flute of champagne waiting for me. The ring on my hand glitters as I grab the drink. I don't look at it...much. It's big and, well, big. Huh.

With the soft blue sapphire halo, the ring is actually really pretty, which surprises me. No sense in over-thinking who chose it or why. I'm the wife of a mob boss. Of course my wedding ring is unique. It's all part of the show.

A flutter of fabric grabs my attention as I sip from the flute. Jessica walks past the table, giving me the barest glance as she beelines for Dante. She's dressed in a faintly yellow strapless gown, the shade so pale it almost looks white. The bodice nips in at the waist, the skirt a double layer of tulle over satin...almost reminiscent of a wedding dress.

Dante moves away before she reaches him, inadvertently leaving her in the dust right when she was about to sidle her way next to him. I smirk to myself and finish off the champagne.

"Looks like you need a refill," a female voice says. "People watching is always more fun with a little alcohol involved, isn't it?"

Glancing up, I'm surprised to see an old classmate from high school, Candi Gallagher, plopping into the chair next to mine. We'd never been close friends, exactly, but she's always been a kind person and her job as a wine acquisitions specialist has brought us together over the years for business. I'm relieved to see her now. Finally, someone who won't put on a false front. I may not know a lot about Candi personally, but she's always been a tell-it-like-it-is person.

"That's true," I agree.

She doesn't hesitate to lift the champagne bottle from the metal ice bucket beside me and refill my glass. "So, do you think she just woke up this morning and decided to wear that getup, or was there some deliberate thought behind it?"

She arches a brow in Jessica's direction.

"Oh, she definitely put some thought into it. That dress is way too close to white to be an accident."

"Well, just goes to show how few brain cells are at work. I hate to bash another woman, but that one's a conniving bitch through and through. I could pass by and accidentally spill a vintage red down her front if you like? Consider it a wedding gift."

Although I have no idea what Jessica could have done to Candi in the past, I'm enjoying this moment of mutually trashing our common enemy. It's good to know it wasn't just my instincts telling me the redhead was bad news. I give a tempted groan.

"I'd love to see that. I would. But I'm sure Dante wouldn't appreciate the ruckus."

Who knows how he'd react to having his mistress called out like that? The thought darkens my mood, so I brush it off.

Candi holds up a bottle of beer. "Cheers to your

wedding, Frankie. And cheers for being a bigger person than me, in refraining from Operation: Ruin the Ho's Dress."

I laugh and clink my glass against her bottle. I'm burning with curiosity about why she's anti-Jessica, but my curiosity will have to wait.

"Whoops. Looks like that's my cue," she says, giving me a nod and departing just as Dante, his brothers, and the rest of the wedding party arrive at the table.

Armani walks over to the emcee and takes the microphone, instructing everyone to have a seat. He drinks casually from a tumbler of whiskey, then goes into an off-the-cuff speech congratulating Dante and me on our wedding. He mentions happiness, longevity, and partnership, as if we've entered into this agreement for any of that. Afterward, Marco takes the mic and regurgitates basically the same thing, only with a charming smile and a dash of humor that has the crowd chuckling.

Listening to the Bellanti brothers speak about me, even in basic terms, is unnerving. They don't know me. I doubt they even remembered my name until today. Dante appears bored with the whole thing. Marco passes the mic down the line to another of their family members.

More words. More congratulations. I guess everyone's just going to blatantly ignore the fact that I was practically sold to the stranger sitting next to me. The words are all dipped in compliments, so thick with praise that I wonder just how long these people have been kissing Dante's ass—you'd think he was some kind of god.

It makes me sick with anger, but I smile the whole time. Even when my face threatens to crack in half.

Just when I think the speeches are never going to end, it's finally over. More wine and champagne are poured, and the waitstaff begin bringing out baskets of rolls and plates of food.

Someone clinks their glass with the side of a spoon and I go still. No, no. I can't handle another publicly inappropriate kiss. But Dante is looking at Jessica, his eyes glued to her as if he's imagining her out of that damn dress. He's oblivious to what the clinking glass represents, or else he's just ignoring it. The noise stops and Dante turns to his meal.

My chest collapses as I squeeze out the breath I'd been holding.

He'd been too busy eye fucking his mistress to kiss me.

Chatter fills the air as everyone dines, and all the while, Dante makes a point of touching me possessively whenever someone comes up to the table to congratulate us. I wish his hands on me weren't such a turn-on.

The minutes pass, and I realize I haven't touched a single bite. Marco leans over to whisper something to Dante, and I catch the phrase "Bruno family" before my husband excuses himself to go attend to some business talk, leaving me alone.

At my side, Charlie sits quietly while Livvie animatedly rattles on about something. She takes Charlie's glass and sneaks a couple sips of wine. I grin as she catches me watching. I widen my eyes at her in faux-shock and she blushes, releases the glass, and goes back to eating.

When Dante returns, the plates are cleared and slices of decadent white cake with raspberry filling are passed around. No official cake cutting for us, I see, though it's probably for the best. My skin heats uncomfortably at the thought of Dante's hand on mine, pressing the knife through the cake, his fingers brushing my lips as he feeds me a bite...

I manage to choke down my cake, taking small bites while I observe my husband, once again casting longing glances at Jessica. Charlie knocks elbows with me and cocks her head.

"Are you going to let this continue on your *wedding* day?"

"What do you suggest I do about it?" I hiss quietly. Do I even want to make a fuss, after he already made it clear he wouldn't be giving up his sidepiece?

I haven't given our wedding night much thought either, mostly because I intend to get it over with as quickly as possible as a matter of formality. His hands on me. His lips cruising my skin. His cock inside me, buried to the hilt as he spills his seed.

A hard shiver courses through my body.

"For one thing, you need to get his attention back on you," Charlie says. "The second thing involves murder, so I won't go there because it wouldn't end well for Jessica."

She's right. I need to get Dante's attention. How does it look to all the folks who just wished us well to have him lusting over his assistant on our wedding day?

Squaring my shoulders, I put my hand on the table and slide it over to his. He reaches for his wineglass before I can touch him. Fine. I'll put my hand on *his* thigh and see how he reacts. Slowly, I reach beneath the table. His leg is close to mine. He could touch me if he wanted to, knee to knee. My fingertips rest against his thigh, softly.

Grow a pair, Frankie.

Bolder. Harder. I press my palm to his leg and curl my fingers against his firm muscle.

Dante turns to me, eyes smoldering. He looks like he's about to say something when there's a crash from the guest area.

My father stands, his chair knocked to the ground, rattling the table with his clumsy movements. My heart sinks. He's drunk. I should have known he was already tipsy when he walked me down the aisle. Of course my soul had known, but I chose to ignore it.

He raises a wineglass in one hand and a beer in the other, then thrusts the wineglass higher. "This is some good shit!"

I move to stand, but Dante stops me with a hand on my arm. Charlie is already on her feet and raises her own glass. "It better be, Dad. We made it!"

The crowd laughs and my sister catches my eye. Leaning over to Dante, I whisper, "I'll take care of this."

Calling up my plastic smile, I grab Charlie's hand and we make our way over to our dad. He stumbles as he weaves his way through the tables, looking for a waiter to refill his glass. Scanning the guests, I realize my mother is nowhere to be found. Of course she's not.

Charlie manages to whisk our dad off and I don't get a chance to make it back to the table before people stop me to talk. Just like that, the meal is officially over, tables are cleared, and a DJ fires up a playlist from a platform in the far corner of the courtyard. Music and alcohol flow freely as I'm bounced inside the jovial crowd, making small talk with people I don't know.

Dante disappears, and it feels like an hour passes before I finally see him in the center of a group of men, talking and laughing. I manage to catch his eye, but he ignores me as he sips from a crystal tumbler. Nonplussed, I find my sisters, relieved when I hear that Charlie stuffed Dad into a car and got him a ride home. Meanwhile Livvie's eyes are sparkling and unfocused, her cheeks flushed. I'm sure she's snuck more than her fair share of wine, but as she twirls off to dance with some friends, I don't chastise her. Let her have her fun, obliviously ignorant to it all.

The party drags on. More wine. More frivolity. The crowd gets louder, more raucous.

Charlie's husband whisks her off to dance, something Dante and I haven't even done. No first dance for us. We've skipped a lot of firsts today, the little details that couples engage in to make the day more special. It's not like we're in this for love, but my husband is doing the bare minimum. I wonder just how much he's going to expect out of me tonight in bed?

Frustrated, I seek him out in the crowd. He's moved

away from the fray to a quieter place on the outskirts where two elaborate brick fireplaces have been lit. Daylight faded a while ago and the flickering flames create a softly glowing ambiance. He's speaking to a trio of men, more of the associates he's spent the whole reception ignoring me in favor of. Though I haven't missed the occasional hungry glances he's given me.

If only he wasn't giving those same looks to Jessica...

Speaking of, the she-devil is right at his side, her elbow touching Dante's. She's closer to him than I've been all day. Dante looks up as if he knows I'm looking—and then he turns away, dismissing me. Again.

Charlie pulls me out on the dance floor with Livvie for one song, then two. I can't stop thinking about tonight, when Dante and I are alone. Maybe there won't be an official wedding night as such. It was never part of the agreement. Maybe we'll wait to cross that bridge until we're ready to produce his heir—

"All right—enough, Frankie. She's all over him."

Charlie tugs me aside and turns me to face Dante. Across the courtyard, I see he's migrated to the other firepit, and Jessica's behind him. Her hands are on his shoulders, kneading, massaging. Eyes half closed, like she's getting off on touching him. My skin crawls.

"March over there and get your man, sis."

Fuck. It's pissing me off that Jessica is pulling this on my wedding day. But I don't really want to stake a claim on him...do I?

"I don't know..." I say, hesitating.

"He's your husband now, Frankie. And he's been

ignoring you all night. MAKE him pay attention to you. You got this."

She's right. My lips tingle with the phantom feel of his mouth pressed there, bruising and punishing, flaming something in me that I'd never felt before.

"Okay. I'm going."

"Good." Charlie grabs me in a fierce hug and squeezes me tight. "Look, we've got to go. I'm going to drop Livvie off at home. But call me tomorrow. I want all the details. Love you."

"Wait, no, you're leaving?"

"It's after midnight, Frankie."

I check the time on my phone—she's right. By now there's only a handful of guests left, and they look pretty firmly entrenched in their conversations.

Livvie rushes over to give me a goodbye hug, and then my sisters head off.

"Love you!" I call after them.

And they're gone. My last tie to myself. Now I'm alone...with the Bellantis.

I snag another glass of wine from a passing waiter and down half of it as I sneak another glance at Dante. He's engrossed in conversation, and appears completely oblivious to Jessica draped all over him. But I'm certainly not oblivious, and though I prefer to keep my life low key, I'm known for pulling out a trick or two when it's called for.

I'm far from drunk, but the few glasses of wine I've had today have made me a little bit loose and a little bit daring. And I'm tired of being shunted out of the spotlight at my own fucking wedding. Enough is enough.

Sham wedding or not, I'm going to make this a night that Dante will never forget.

With a bit of maneuvering, I manage to unzip my dress, feeling only a fraction of regret for dropping the confectionary beauty of my dress on the ground.

Lifting my chin, I carefully step out of it, knowing my white lace basque, matching garter set, and satin stilettos show off all my assets to great advantage.

I stride over to my husband, the sight of me in my strappy corset ensemble stopping any conversations dead in their tracks.

Warm air caresses my bare flesh, a slight breeze threading through my hair as I approach Dante. His acquaintances notice me before he does, staring at me open-mouthed. Jessica jolts, her jaw dropping as I saunter past her and reach for Dante's arm.

His face is impenetrable granite as he finally notices me. Undeterred, I grab him by the edge of his undone bow tie.

"I believe you have some business to conclude, Mr. Bellanti."

The corners of his delectable lips jerk up in what might have been a smile had he let it bloom. Instead, he nods to his associates.

"Excuse me, gentlemen. Stay as long as you like, but I'm turning in for the night."

9

FRANKIE

Leading my new husband away from the firepit and toward the Bellanti estate, I quickly realize what an amateurish move I've just made: I don't actually know where his room is.

Dante walks slightly behind me, allowing me to put on a show of leading him by his tie, but I start to slow down as we reach the back of the house.

Before I can turn around, Dante solves the problem by scooping me up unceremoniously and carrying me inside. His face is a mixture of amusement with a touch of annoyance. Seriously? Is this a chore for him? Most men trip over themselves at any opportunity for sex, and he's acting like I've inconvenienced him.

Stopping a moment to kick the door closed behind us, he strides down the hall as if I weigh nothing in his arms.

"That was a neat little power play there, Francesca."

He hasn't even glanced at my breasts—and it's not like he can miss them popping over the top of my corset.

I bristle. "That's not my name."

Dante takes a left. The halls are dark, rich wood paneling, the floor, beautifully neutral slabs of stone. "It's the name on the contract I signed. Francesca Carina Abriana Abbott...Bellanti. So many lovely names and you choose to go by *Frankie*."

How rude can he be? "That's right. So get used to it."

"Never."

He adjusts his grip on me to open a door, then carries me inside and locks it behind us.

The room is cavernous and richly appointed with carved furniture and sumptuous fabrics, though I can't see much detail since a small lamp on the nightstand provides the only light.

Without another word, Dante tosses me onto the massive bed and flicks his tie onto the floor. My eyes track his body, the lines of his broad chest and muscular arms beneath his tux. The promise of a tight abdomen. The impressive bulge in the front of his pants.

Oh my God.

I'd thought he wasn't interested in doing this—that we'd be merely going through the motions—yet he's sporting an erection that clearly says otherwise. My chest wells with satisfaction, and I feel a quick surge of feminine power seeing the proof of his lust. I guess I do have something over him after all. He's attracted to me. He wants me.

Dante slips out of his tux jacket and tosses it onto the floor as if the expensive fabric means nothing. Next are his cufflinks, those big hands and their strong fingers working the little gold adornments loose. Dropping them onto the nightstand, he slips out of his vest and begins to unbutton his shirt. I'm pretty sure the mass pressing against his zipper just got bigger. I grin a little. I'll have him eating out of my hand in no time.

Now that he's disrobing, and it's clear that this is actually happening, I've lost some of my resolve—but the lust coursing through me makes up for it. My body thrums with charged, sexual heat. My thong is getting wetter by the second as I watch him undress piece by piece. Taking my cue, I sit and reach behind me to tug the stays that hold the corset together.

I've barely gotten the ribbons loose when Dante stops me, pulling my hands away and shoving me back down on the bed. My breath hitches as he pins my wrists above my head with one hand, his face lowering over mine. Tingles race over my skin, my pulse jacking even higher at his dominance. He leans close, as if he's going to say something in my ear—but instead he grips my chin, crushing his mouth against mine.

The warmth of his tongue invades me, and a gasp strangles in my throat as his weight presses me into the mattress. My lips throb from the memory of our kiss earlier, the pulse between my legs beating with demand. But this time is different. This kiss is harsher, more aggressive. Dante doesn't hold anything back.

Still trapping me with his body, he grinds the kiss into me harder, claiming my mouth completely, flaming pleasure with every slight twist of his head and movement of his lips. His other hand roughly pulls the half-loose corset down, over my breasts and hips, where it gets stuck. With a grunt, he pulls away from me and rips the delicate fabric right in two, impatiently whipping the lingerie across the room. My breasts bounce from the movement, drawing his gaze. I touch my swollen lips, wondering if they're bruised from his kiss.

Dante moves over me again to unclasp my stockings from the garter. Then he hooks a finger around the crotch of my thong, his knuckle brushing my pussy lips, so he can pull my underwear off in one rough tug. Adrenaline pumps through me, my breath coming faster. My husband doesn't look me in the eye as he whisks off my garter and then my heels, leaving only my stockings, and climbs back on top of me.

Tingles of pleasure bombard me, darting between my legs. I've never felt so naked. Dante is still in his shirt and pants and I arch against him, all my most sensitive places rubbing up against the fine fabric and his muscular body beneath. I'm unable to stop myself as a gasp works free from my lips.

Shame heats my cheeks as I realize how turned on I am. What the hell is wrong with me?

I don't even know this man. I was *forced* to marry him —and he's acting like a total barbarian. But none of those things are enough to keep me from lusting after him.

Dante leans back, hot gaze raking over my body, as if he's taking inventory of his new wife. Judging by the hungry look in his eyes, he likes what he sees. I swivel my hips a little, trying to be alluring. Letting him know I'm ready for him.

He just smirks at me, tracing the lacy elastic bands that keep my stockings tight around my thighs.

"Are you a virgin, Francesca?"

I stop moving. "I don't see why—"

"Are you, or not?" His tone hardens, as if he's losing patience with me.

"No." I shoot him a glare, but he ignores it.

"How many men?"

He's toying with me, getting back at me for maneuvering him away from his friends and Jessica earlier. He wants the power back. I prop myself up on my elbows and level him with my most eat-shit-and-die look.

"Dozens. I couldn't keep track."

A liquid smile crosses his lips, slow, taunting. "Liar."

He slides to the floor and removes his shirt, then his undershirt, revealing a broad, muscular chest lightly dusted with dark hair that trails over his tight abdomen and down toward the bulge in his pants. He's out of those in an instant, and now I can't stop staring at his body. This man is pure perfection. My fingers itch to run over the dips and rises sculpting his middle, to squeeze the firmness of his biceps. Before I can reach for him, Dante is back on the bed, his strong hands spreading my thighs wide open.

"Wait," I pant, looking up at him in a panic. "Don't you need to get a condom?"

"I expect an heir, a stipulation you agreed to," Dante says flatly. "The sooner the better."

"But—"

I barely have time to process what's happening before

he plunges into me without preamble. Hard and deep. To the hilt. Luckily, I'm already soaking wet, but the fullness of his thick cock has me gasping.

Shocked that he's entered me like this, without foreplay, without any tenderness, I pull in a breath and lift my hips to meet his long, forceful thrusts. He's using me hard, clearly not interested in my pleasure, but God—his dick is hitting all the right places without him even trying. Pleasure hums through my center, despite the obvious lack of affection.

Gripping his shoulders tight, I clamp my thighs around his hips, drawing him in deeper and holding him in place to keep the pleasure going. A familiar, swirling pressure builds, shocking me to my core. How can the sex feel this good when there aren't any feelings between us?

His eyes meet mine, but I can tell he doesn't really see me. He's a million miles away. And so am I. Refusing to give him the satisfaction of hearing me moan, I squeeze my eyes shut as an impending orgasm starts to flood every inch of me. I try to will it away, but there's no stopping it. My hips grind into his even faster, and he answers with a hard, insistent, raw thrust that sends me right over the edge.

Hating myself for the whimper that leaves my throat, I dig my nails into his flesh as I come. The contractions are so hard, I know there's no way Dante can mistake what's happening.

Opening my eyes, I find he looks surprised that I'm coming beneath him. For some reason, it only makes him even more possessive. He growls and dips his lips to my neck, trailing kisses down to my chest, nipping me with his teeth as he drives himself into me like a wild man.

My orgasm is fading, but it doesn't go away as he pounds against that sweet spot deep inside, flaming the pleasure all over again. Biting and sucking my breasts as he thrusts. Hard and deep, faster and faster, until I can't keep myself from crying out. All I can do is hang on.

"Fuck yes," he groans against my neck. His cock stiffens a second before he pumps his release into me, pushing me to orgasm once more. I can't hold back the moans this time.

Dante relaxes on top of me, his limbs entangled with mine. His weight is pushing me down on the mattress in the most delicious way. My arms instinctively go around his waist, and my pussy clenches around him with after-shocks of pleasure as I hold him close. My mind is in a haze. I can't believe what just happened.

I've had sex plenty of times before, but it hadn't been anything like that. At all.

Suddenly Dante pushes himself up on his elbows and looks down at me. I have no idea what he's thinking, if I'm being met with his approval or his scorn. Damn his granite face.

Before I can think of anything to say, he rolls off the bed, his semi-hard cock glistening and proud as he grabs his pants and pulls them back on. He slips his shirt on next, leaving the buttons undone.

"You must have learned some good tricks from the 'dozens' of men you've slept with," he says nonchalantly.

I sit up and try to gather my dignity around me, along

with the bed sheet. Dante ignores me, picking up the rest of his clothes and avoiding eye contact. A chill races down my back.

"Enjoy your rooms." He gives me the absolute barest of glances before turning to the door. "Your clothes are in the closet and the en suite is fully stocked. Feel free to decorate however you like."

And then he's gone, leaving me alone in what I've just realized is *my* bedroom, not his. Sinking back onto the bed, my body still trembles from his touch, still burns from the power of our mutual release. I stare up at the white ceiling, mind racing.

My sister said I could have him eating out of the palm of my hand. Just warm his bed, let him underestimate me, and he'd let me do whatever I want.

A harsh laugh bubbles from my throat. I can't believe I thought I could control Dante Bellanti with my body. The thought is a fucking joke now.

I'm in way over my head.

10

FRANKIE

Morning comes, and I'm surprised to realize I slept soundly after Dante left me alone.

Sitting up in the massive bed, I shield my eyes from the brilliant sunlight streaming in through the windows and give myself a few seconds to adjust. My body aches all over, but the insides of my thighs are the worst. I'm sure if I looked in a mirror, I'd find bruises from the hard, demanding way Dante took me. I flush just thinking about it. It's still hard to believe that this is reality. My new reality.

I'm a Bellanti now.

Which means that today, I'll get an inside look at Bellanti Vineyards—one of the most successful wineries in all of California, if not the world.

The place must run like a well-oiled machine to have achieved such success. I want to know every operational detail, see every step of the process. They might be raking in the profits, but even so, I know there has to be room for improvement. I'll assess the winery's strengths and weaknesses initially, then determine how to restructure operations and maximize efficiency. I learned plenty about those things in Tuscany, and I'm dying to put my new knowledge to use. Even if it is for the benefit of the Bellantis, the idea flat out thrills me.

Granted, I haven't been officially welcomed into the business. *Yet*. I need to learn the lay of the land first, so to speak, then show how I can be of value. But I'm confident I'll work my way into a position promptly. No way am I sitting on my hands all day, wishing away the time when I can be actively working.

At least this sham of a marriage will allow me to pursue my passion.

I slide onto the floor. The marble is cool beneath my soles and a shiver of exhilaration goes through me. I never sleep late. My internal clock chimes shortly after sunrise every day unless I'm sick or exhausted from stretching myself too thin. Considering the long day I had, thanks to the wedding and the reception (and the even longer night, leaving me with just a few hours' sleep), I *should* be exhausted. But I'm not. I feel invigorated.

After showering in my extremely luxurious new en suite, I blow out my hair before twisting it into a professional bun at the nape of my neck. A few loose strands hang around my face, and I leave them to soften my appearance. I don't want to seem uptight or intimidating to any new-to-me people I'll meet today.

I give my mostly empty walk-in closet careful consideration, then dress in a smart gray suit. The jacket hugs my waist and has a feminine curve to the lapels, but the suit is completely office appropriate. I pair it with a white blouse and simple black heels. No jewelry save for my wedding band, and just enough makeup to give me some color. Assessing myself in the closet's floor-length mirror, I tame my excitement as my stomach rumbles. It's been quite a long time since I've eaten.

Unfortunately, I hardly know the layout of this massive building. Hell, I could probably get lost inside my bedroom suite if I actually wandered around it. The scent of coffee is easy to follow, though, and I make my way down the hall and into the room it's coming from. Two men in white aprons go wide-eyed as I stride in. I quickly realize I've entered the kitchen. Everything is stainless steel and commercial grade, and while the quick peek I take says it's impressive, the look on the chef's face says I'm not supposed to be here.

"Oh, I'm sorry." I turn to leave.

"Madam," he says, his words slightly French-accented, "if you would take a seat in the dining room, I'll be glad to prepare your order."

I arch my brows. "My order?"

The chef nods. He's an older man with a tuft of silver and black hair curling from beneath his white chef's hat. "Yes, Mrs. Bellanti. What would you like?"

A slow grin spreads across my face. No more microwavable egg sandwiches for me! I don't know why I was surprised—of course the Bellantis can afford a personal chef.

He must see the impressed and slightly greedy gleam in my eye, because he looks amused now. "Anything you can imagine. I enjoy a challenge," he teases. "Something en flambé, perhaps? Paella? Macarons? Consommé?"

"I'd love a Tuscan omelet," I tell him. "I really miss the food I had when I was in Italy."

"Beautiful. Sun dried tomatoes, olives, artichoke hearts, prosciutto?"

"Yes, yes, yes, and yes. All of it."

The corners of his eyes crinkle as if he's enjoying this. "Mozzarella, pecorino, asiago?"

"All the cheeses, yes, a thousand times yes," I say, trying not to drool. "And toast—the crustiest rustic bread you have, browned until it's crispy."

"It will be...most crisp," he says seriously.

"With real butter on top, and fruit on the side," I go on gluttonously. "Any fruit is good. Whatever's on hand."

He's nodding along with all my requests. "Of course. Coffee?"

"Black, dark roast please."

"Excellent." He gestures toward a door to his left. "The dining room, Mrs. Bellanti. Your meal will be out shortly."

"Perfect. And your name is?"

"Alain," he answers.

I nod. "Thank you, Alain. I'm Frankie."

He leads the way, opening the door for me. Then he gives a little bow as I walk through, retreating back to the kitchen and leaving me in an imposing room with two Bellanti men staring at me from their places at the table.

Everything in here is mahogany—the massive table that seats twelve, the wainscoting, the carved sideboard. Dark green curtains stand guard over the windows, a triple bowl chandelier casting dim artificial light. The table is set with fine china that has a flourish of gold patterning around the edges, crystal glassware, polished silver cutlery. I take it all in before I notice my husband's raised brow. Armani is seated across from him, looking far less intimidating.

"What a pleasant surprise," Armani says mildly. "You're up early."

"I always am," I say.

"I figured we'd see Marco at breakfast before we saw you," Dante adds, seeming less than thrilled at my presence. "Though he's apparently still holed up in his room with a woman—possibly two—so I'm sure he's in no hurry."

I'm frozen to the spot, not wanting to sit down next to my husband. I see he's rolled out of bed today still an asshole. Maybe I should just turn around and leave. Dante must sense my hesitation, because he reaches over and pulls out the chair next to him. I guess I have no choice.

"You didn't have to go to all this trouble just for me," I say, sitting down gingerly and scooting myself closer to the table. "The formal setting, the fine china, it's a bit much—"

"We didn't." Dante takes a sip of his coffee, looking incredibly bored. "This is just breakfast."

"Oh."

My entire face goes hot, my hairline itching. I let this man fuck me last night? Granted, I more or less expected that he'd treat me like this. I don't know why I'm so embarrassed by it.

Armani glares at Dante as he leaves his seat to come around the table and pour coffee from a silver carafe into my cup. I'm not expecting that at all, and it takes my brain a second to recognize his kindness.

"Sugar or cream?" he asks, gesturing at a small silver pitcher and a dish of sugar cubes.

"Just black is great, actually." I smile at him gratefully, sipping my coffee as quietly as possible. I'm careful not to let my arm brush against Dante. "Thank you."

"You're welcome." Armani slides back into his chair, his eyes flicking to Dante again, this time with a hint of reprimand. "This was one of our father's traditions, actually. To start the day with the best and expect nothing less for the rest of the day. Lunch is much less formal."

I force a little laugh in an attempt to shrug off my lingering humiliation. "Given how successful your winery is, I can't fault the logic. Your father must have been onto something."

"He certainly was," Armani says.

Dante huffs out a breath, but he seems to be ignoring both of us now. How charming.

I'd love to ask him what crawled up his ass, but I bite

my tongue. Maybe he's always like this. Luckily, my food arrives before I attempt any further small talk, on a plate with a silver dome over the top. The other man in the white apron—Alain's assistant, perhaps—sets the plate down and removes the dome, revealing a picture-perfect dish that could easily be the cover of a food magazine. The aroma of sharp pecorino and sundried tomato, melted butter, and sliced melon makes my stomach clench with anticipation.

"Thank you," I murmur dreamily. "This looks amazing."

The man nods and refills my coffee before departing. I lay my napkin over my lap, ready to dig in.

That's when I notice my husband looking at me from the corner of his eye, but I don't acknowledge it. He probably has something to say about the huge spread in front of me, but he can stuff it. I'm hungry and not one to pass up the talents of a personal chef.

I take my first forkful and my mouth has an orgasm. This is easily the most delicious omelet I've ever eaten. The prosciutto practically brings a tear to my eye, and the toast is so crisp that I don't even care I'm scattering crumbs all over myself with every crunchy bite. The food is more than enough to distract me from the awkwardness I feel around Dante, and thank God.

Armani picks up where the brothers apparently left off in their conversation before I arrived—something to do with purchase orders and inventory barcodes. I could probably catch on, but I'm too absorbed in my meal to bother. However, I do notice that Dante hasn't touched a lick of food since I arrived. He's nursing his coffee and checking his phone as he gives his brother partial attention. Soon, Armani puts his napkin down and sets his fork on his plate. Realizing they're about to leave, I take a few final, hurried bites. Dante gets to his feet first, then his brother. I take a last swig of coffee, wipe my mouth on my napkin, and stand, too.

They're halfway to the door when Dante gives me a sharp glance over his shoulder, realizing I'm behind them. He stops in his tracks, turning to face me.

"What are you doing?"

I narrow my eyes. "Heading into the office, obviously."

Dante smirks. "You don't work for Bellanti Vineyards."

I don't find anything funny about the sarcastic amusement in his voice. "Well, maybe not yet, but I—"

He turns away from me and straightens the cuffs of his bespoke suit jacket. "Bellanti women don't have to pretend to work for their money. You'll find a credit card on your dresser." Looking my elegant suit up and down, he adds, "Buy something more appropriate to wear."

With that, he strides out the door.

My eyes sting. Armani is still here, so I hold it together. His brown eyes are soft, apologetic even.

"You just got married, Francesca. Maybe take some time for yourself today, buy some nice things. It's okay to spoil yourself a little. You deserve it for putting up with him."

He winks and then leaves, the door closing with a soft click that seems to echo in the huge dining room. Steeped in humiliation and grappling with a hurricane of emotions, I stare blankly at the door. I hate my husband. I detest him. He might claim ownership of my body, but he'll never have more of me than that.

Armani is right. I'm going to have to put up with Dante for the rest of my life. I might as well take advantage of the situation however I can.

And I'm going to start by finishing my breakfast.

FRANKIE

DANTE'S GOING to pay for his comment about my "inappropriate" attire.

It's now my mission to find out how long it takes to max out a credit card. I'm hoping a few solid hours of nonstop shopping will do it, but I'm willing to go to more extreme efforts if that doesn't do the trick.

I'm going to make my husband regret ever giving me this platinum card. He thinks my clothes are too outdated? Fine. His eyes are going to cross and his bank account is going to cry when he sees the amount of clothing I bring home. And I'm not stopping there. Oh no. He wants me to be a proper Bellanti wife? I'm going all out.

All. Out.

Because fuck him.

I change into a flouncy red sundress with a slim gold belt around the middle, a pair of Italian leather sandals, and a floppy hat, and then head downstairs to go about getting a ride to my father's house so I can pick up my car. If it's still there, that is. I know my father is desperate enough to have tried selling it, but I'm not sure how many buyers would line up to make an offer on a shitty 1994 Volkswagen Golf with a sticky manual transmission. Honestly, I'm not even sure the engine will turn over for me after three years of sitting abandoned in the back of the garage, but it's worth a try. With a car, at least I'd have a little freedom.

One of the staff members is dusting the sideboard in the hall, and gives me a confused look when I mention what I need.

"Mr. Bellanti has made Donovan available for all your transportation needs today, Mrs. Bellanti."

"Great. Except I don't know who Donovan is or how to find him. Do you maybe have a number where I can reach him, or...?"

Her cheeks go a little pink, as if she's embarrassed on my behalf. I mean, I'm just the wife whose husband has told her absolutely zero about how his household is run. I'm sure there are a hundred things at my disposal that I'll never know about until I suss them out on my own. Dante can't be bothered, obviously.

My wedding ring should have come with an instruction manual.

"I—no. Donovan is the family driver, Mrs. Bellanti. There's no need to call. I just saw him in the kitchen having coffee. I'll fetch him for you."

She hurries off before I can thank her, a man appearing much quicker than I would have imagined for a man enjoying his coffee. I suppose being at the beck and call of this family requires superhuman response times to a summons, or else.

The man gives a little bow, his dark hair graying at the temples. His face is pleasant, with deep crow's feet beside brown eyes suggesting years of constant smiling. He looks around my dad's age, but a bit on the sturdy side. Something about him makes me feel I'm in good hands.

"Mrs. Bellanti. Very pleased to formally meet you. Where may I take you today?"

"I just need a ride to my father's so I can pick up my car. I have some errands to run."

His head dips respectfully. "No need to drive yourself. I'm at your service for the day. Mr. Bellanti would insist, of course."

Like I care. "Thank you for the offer, but I'd really like to drive myself."

His smile tightens though his eyes are indomitably kind. "Mr. Bellanti *would insist*, Madam."

I hear what he's not saying: *Don't stir the pot, Mrs. Bellanti*.

Fine. I'll play by Dante's rules. For now.

"Okay. I'd like to go to Union Square, please. I'm all ready to go," I say.

"Very good. This way."

An hour later, we arrive at the best shopping district in San Francisco. Donovan drops me off and gives me his cell number so I can call when I'm done. All the shops are within easy walking distance, so I can browse the day away at my leisure. I've only gone a block when I find a shop full of couture, with designer names on the window that I've never even heard of. One look as I step inside, and I know I haven't heard of them because they aren't the mainstream chic that everyone knows about. These are the subtle designers that rich people pay huge money to wear while trying to keep it quiet so they don't have to share with the masses.

I approach the registers and ask for a stylist. The sales associate gives me a blasé look while she slips a blouse onto a hanger, sets it down slowly, and smiles like she doesn't mean it. Her gaze sweeps over me and it's all very *Pretty Woman* as she clearly dismisses me by picking up another shirt and hanger.

"You can have a seat and I'll see if someone is available." She gestures weakly to a velvet chair in the corner. "Name?"

I give my best Julia Roberts, "bless your heart" smile. "Mrs. Dante Bellanti, but you can call me Francesca."

The hanger drops from her hand and clatters across the countertop. "Just a moment, please. Can I get you a sparkling water? Some champagne? I'm Marin, by the way."

I don't sit. Instead I wait by the counter, leaning against it like I own the place. If I have to be married to a giant asshat, I might as well take advantage of his name and live up to it.

A perky blonde comes over with a big to-do, air kisses my cheeks, and ushers me to a plush fitting room for measurements.

"What are we looking for today?" she asks. "Something for a special event, or...?"

I tell her I need an entire work wardrobe, and her eyes light up.

The array of outfits she selects make me giddy. Professional suits with exactly the right details, like belted silk jackets or slightly puffed shoulder seams. Perfectly tapered pencil skirts, blouses with hand embroidered cuffs, wide leg trousers and matching vests with a hint of masculine flare. There are dresses stylish enough for the office, but flirty enough to transition to dinner wear. And so many scarves, shoes, and other accessories that it makes my head spin.

I spend the next hour trying things on, while my new friends—Tina and Marin—lavish me with compliments and champagne and so much flattery I have to beg them to stop.

Every time I come across an article of clothing that makes me feel like I can conquer the world, I buy it...in two or three colors. Tina convinces me to wear one of my new skirt suits out the door, so I choose a summer weight linen and a sassy pair of snakeskin high-heeled sandals to go with it. I have to admit, I look like a million bucks. After I pay, I tell Marin to hold my bags until my driver Donovan shows up to collect them. She's very accommodating.

The next uber exclusive boutique I swan into specializes in lingerie. I'm not sure if it's the new suit or if I'm projecting some kind of haughty, newfound confidence, but this time there's not a moment's hesitation from the sales staff when they see me coming. They're on me like flies on honey, showing me the most expensive frilly, slinky, and sexy things on the racks.

This is a whole new world for me. I've never gone out of my way to purchase sexy underthings. Practical suits me better. I suppose I never understood the necessity of lace floss for underwear. Yet as I run my hands over the frothy bras and panties, I'm starting to get it. I stock up on the sexiest underwear and sleepwear I can find, including a gorgeous sheer dressing gown in pale lavender with yards of fluffy marabou trim. I also get a pair of ridiculous open-toed slippers with kitten heels and a fuzzy ball on top, just because.

I have to send Donovan back to the house with all my bags and boxes when I'm done, because I'm nowhere near finished with my shopstravaganza, and I literally wouldn't fit in the back seat with my haul.

While I wait for him to get back, I stroll through more shops, picking up a few other things here and there—a bag of chocolate-covered strawberries from a boutique candy shop, which I eat promptly, Diamonds by the Yard necklaces from Tiffany for me and my sisters, and a jaunty new hat for Donovan to express my appreciation. The sun is out, everything is brilliant and fresh, and I feel a little content. Happy, even? It's the thrill of spending Dante's money, and I'm not done yet.

Rounding a corner at the end of the block, I spy a small classic car dealership tucked in between a coffee shop and yet another jewelry store. I wouldn't give it a second thought normally, but I spy a cherry red Jaguar parked at the end of the lot, the crimson paint glistening in the sunlight. It sparkles a little, like it's calling me over. It's a sign. I have to go look.

Turns out Ms. Cherry is a two-seater convertible with buttery soft dark tan leather, a glossy wooden steering wheel, and burlwood console accents.

"Mrs. Dante Bellanti." I give the salesperson my hand for a firm shake, my huge wedding ring glinting, and that's all it takes to get me a test drive.

My heart flips as I zip around, the engine purring like a content kitten. If there's one way to blow up a credit card, this little beauty will do the trick. Plus, I love it. Pulling into the dealership once again, I send Donovan a text that I've got a ride home. I do some paperwork, pay with my new card, and wink at my beauty of a car before slipping into the driver's seat.

I'm about to pull away when my phone rings. It's a customer service rep, calling from American Express. *Finally.* I'd been wondering how long it would take to hear from them. After the introductory spiel, I have to verify some information so they know it's really me.

"Thank you, Mrs. Bellanti. The reason we're calling is because we're concerned about some recent activity—"

"All me," I say jauntily, cutting the guy off. "I'm just having a little shopping day."

"I see. Well, we'd just like to inform you that you've nearly reached the limit on your card."

I gasp lightly. I'm such a good actress. "I have a *limit?*"

There's a pause, and he clears his throat, as if trying

to find just the right words. "Yes, ma'am, you do. Let's see...it appears that Mr. Bellanti arranged a credit line of...$100,000, which means that your available balance remaining is...$223.39," he says, respectfully if somewhat nervously. "We *can* increase your credit line, of course, but we'll need the primary account holder to call us in order to get that approved."

"Perfect. I'll take it up with my husband," I say breezily.

Dang, I'm good. I thank the man for his time and hang up. I can't wait to give my sisters their necklaces, and show off my car. I keep the top down, letting the wind whip my hair as I drive to Charlie's house in Nob Hill. I park, let myself in, and find Livvie in Charlie's studio.

Both of my sisters sit near the windows, easels in front of them, their backs to the door as they work in the natural light. Charlie's painting a portrait of Livvie that already seems to capture her inner glow. Livvie is sketching one of her horses, per usual, and I can see a few reference photos clipped to the top of her easel. I stride into the room with the turquoise Tiffany & Co. bags in my hand, and they gasp to see me so unexpectedly.

"I come bearing gifts," I sing out.

"From *Tiffany*?" Livvie squeals. "Oh my God, and is that a new suit? It's gorgeous!"

"It is. Now, I have one for you, and one for you, and one for me. I feel like Oprah!" I pass out the bags. Livvie dives into hers immediately, and the second she gets her box open she starts cooing at the sparkling diamond necklace.

Charlie's jaw drops when she sees it. "Are you kidding? Five thousand dollars?"

I peer into Livvie's box with a frown. "Forty-nine-hundred, technically. But that wasn't supposed to be in there." I snatch the little tag out.

Charlie raises a brow. Her box is still in her hand. "What's this all about?"

I shrug. "Dante insulted my wardrobe, so I did a little shopping. At his expense."

My sister's expression immediately turns to one of approval. "Good girl!"

She does a little dance as she unboxes her necklace and immediately puts it on. Soon, all three of us are wearing our matching necklaces and feeling fabulous.

My cell rings just as we're about to take a selfie. It's Dante.

I smirk, hit ignore, and go back to the photo session. He's probably calling about the credit card. Perhaps he's regretting his instructions to me this morning. Live and learn, sucka.

Determined not to let him interrupt my afternoon with my sisters, I order us Thai delivery for lunch and we sit in the sunroom to eat. It's a delight. Not how I was expecting to spend my day, considering I'd gotten up with the intention of going to work. But this is so much better.

Before I realize it, the afternoon is gone and Livvie is ready to go home. She'd spent the night with Charlie to avoid being alone in the house with our drunk, belligerent father. Smart decision. I wish I could bring her home with me and have her stay forever. It doesn't sit right with either me or Charlie that Livvie is alone with our dad's unpredictable mean streak, but her horses are there and she's adamant that she be there to feed and care for them.

"I'll drive you back," I offer.

She claps her hands. "Only if we go the long way so I can get a decent ride in the Jag!"

"Deal. And I know it needs work, but since I have a new car, the Golf is yours, Livvie."

The room goes silent. Glancing at Charlie first, Livvie gives me an apologetic half-smile.

"What?" I ask.

"The VW's...gone," Livvie says gently. "Dad junked it a few years ago—I think he got a few hundred dollars for it."

Charlie adds, "I'm so sorry. I know it was your baby."

I feel a sting, the unexpected loss of something I was once so attached to and so proud of. I bought that car with my own money, taught myself to drive on that stick shift. And now it's just...gone. Because of our father. "Well," I say, forcing myself to sound cheery. "I guess the Jag is a pretty good consolation prize, right?"

"Definitely," Livvie agrees. "Let's go!"

We take the scenic route through Marin County, soaking up winding roads lined with leafy old trees, and carefully manicured neighborhoods, and finally, the Golden Gate Bridge. The fading sun looks magical in the shimmer of the water, and traffic is light so I can zip along while Livvie waves her arms above her head, her hair flying around in the wind. We both laugh and whoop as we clear the bridge. This is a beautiful memory I'll hold on to for the rest of my life.

We're cruising down the narrow highway toward Napa when my phone rings. Dante, again. I hit ignore, again. Livvie looks at me in shock, her eyes widening.

"Shouldn't you—?"

"So," I say in my best big sister sing-song voice. "Tell me about your latest crush."

Her forehead scrunches. "Boys? I don't have time for boys. You know that."

"Of course you do. Look at you. I bet they're lined up on their knees begging and pleading for just one date."

"You're *so* right," she teases. "My new crush is Marco Bellanti. He *did* ask me to dance at the wedding, you know. He was completely smitten after I stepped on his fancy shoes."

We laugh, both of us well aware that Livvie—for all her youth and passion—is way too smart to get caught up with a player like Marco. But my good humor is tainted by the sobering knowledge that if I hadn't left Italy, my baby sister would be the one with Dante's credit card. The one dealing with a hellish homelife, and a husband who didn't care about her.

As we cross into Napa Valley, the temperature rises slightly, the air humid with a familiar weight and a mineral scent. I look in my rearview mirror and see storm clouds gathering in the distance. I should probably pull over and put the top up just to be safe, so we don't get rained on, but nah. I'll risk it. We're almost home and the clouds still look pretty far off.

Just then, my phone rings. Probably Dante again. I ignore it, but Livvie grabs it from the center console and answers, pulling away when I reach for it.

"No, this is her sister," she says. "Who's calling, please?"

She makes eyes at me again and covers the phone speaker with her hand. "Who's Rico?"

I swerve a little, catch myself, and settle back into my lane. Snatching the phone from my sister, I give it a nonchalant toss over the side of my door, letting it clatter onto the highway.

"Oops, dropped the call."

Livvie is aghast. "Frankie! That's your phone!"

"Hey, no talking *to* boys. Only about them."

"I can't believe you just did that!"

I can't believe I did that. Gripping the wheel, I will my racing heart to slow down and hope like hell nothing shows on my face.

"You are a total badass!" Livvie says, and I can't help but laugh along with her.

Until the shrill whoop of a siren cuts our laughter short.

Red and blue lights flash in my rearview mirror. There's a police car behind us.

Shit.

1 2

FRANKIE

A COP MUST HAVE SEEN me toss the phone. We're in Napa, so littering is a serious offense around here. Guess my new rich husband can pay for my ticket, then.

I pull over and have Livvie pass me the vehicle registration from the glovebox. I also have a fresh printout of my new insurance cards, luckily, which the dealer required for the sale.

The officer looks serious as he approaches, aviator sunglasses giving him an intimidating Terminator vibe. "License, registration, and proof of insurance, ma'am."

I hand everything over with a warm smile that he doesn't return. His thin lips pull into a disquieting, knowing kind of smirk as he scans the brand-new paperwork.

"Remain in your vehicle, please."

He goes back to his cruiser and my nerves jump. Crap. What if the insurance didn't go through? Or maybe the AmEx charge was somehow declined after all and the dealer wanted the car back.

"Oh my God, Frankie!" Livvie whispers in that disbelieving, teenager way.

"It'll be fine."

"We're going to jail!" she teases. "You think their cafeteria has vegan options?"

I force a smile at her good-natured ribbing, but inside I have a bad feeling.

A few moments later, the officer returns with my paperwork.

"Your husband is waiting for you at home, little lady. Go on."

Little lady? Ugh. Despite my irritation, I keep my face neutral. "You're...not going to give me a ticket?"

He smiles, but that somehow makes it all worse. "Drop your sister off and get home. Now."

I'm completely baffled at how this cop knows Livvie is my sister, and that Dante wants me home, but I just nod and thank him. Jesus, my husband has everyone in his back pocket. And it seems he can track me down, no matter what I'm doing.

I drive off, cracking a joke to my sister about how good it is to have a well-connected husband. But meanwhile, my knuckles are white on the steering wheel.

————

THE WIND IS HOWLING like mad by the time I get back to the Bellanti estate and park behind the massive house, quickly raising the convertible top. Thank goodness a push button makes quick work of securing the roof, because the first fat drops of rain begin to fall just as I step out of the vehicle. A crack of thunder booms in my ears as I turn to race for the door.

And run smack into my husband.

His hand goes around my upper arm like a vice grip and he levels me with an expression I have no trouble reading. Rage. It matches the ominous atmosphere so well he could be elemental himself—dark eyes flashing, angry energy swirling around him like the wind.

I liked it better when he had his poker face on. At least then I didn't know I was in for it.

"Pick up the fucking phone when I call you."

My eyes narrow, but inside I shiver, hard and deep. The fear crawls across my skin, instinctual, leaving gooseflesh in its wake. I've been pretty defiant all day about making him pay for insulting me, though that defiance was laced with a trepidation that I pushed aside. Now all those nerves come to the surface, and I'm wary of what Dante is going to do next.

Being his wife, I'd assumed he wouldn't get physical with me—but maybe I was wrong. Still, I won't let him see that I'm afraid. Considering the kind of man he is, it might just spur him to violence. So I lift my chin and glare right back, even though we're getting pelted by rain.

"My father may have sold me off to you, but you don't own every minute of my time. Besides, my phone had an unfortunate accident on the freeway. I'm going to need a new one."

When I smirk, his eyes narrow, his grip tightening on my arm. It should be painful. It is painful. But it's arousing me, and I hate it. I don't want to feel turned on by this.

"Don't act like a stupid bitch, Francesca."

"Then stop being such a controlling asshole, *Dante*."

He shoves me back against the car hard enough that the thud can be heard over the harsh wind. "You have no fucking clue who I am, do you?" he growls.

"Oh, here we go with your ego."

We're going to get soaked, and my new linen skirt suit will be ruined. How much longer is he going to keep me out here? I'm about to lay into the arrogant prick properly when he leans low over me, pinning me back against the hood, cutting me off before I can open my mouth.

He grips my chin, forcing me to look at him.

"I'm the first son of Enzo Bellanti. I dine with criminals and senators at the same table. I drink with mobsters and the occasional prince. I know dangerous people and I've made dangerous enemies. Enemies who would love nothing more than to cut my pretty new wife's throat from ear to ear, just to take her from me."

His hand trails beneath my chin to the center of my throat, where he lightly traces his thumb across.

"Is that supposed to be a threat from you, or from them?" It was supposed to sound sarcastic, but my voice comes out too softly.

The rain starts pouring down in earnest now, more thunder rumbling ominously in the distance, but Dante doesn't take his eyes from me. His hand is still wrapped around my throat, leaving my neck tingling. As I look up at him he consumes me with his heat and his dominance, as if ingraining into me that he very much controls every inch of me.

"Don't worry," he says, blocking the rain from my face. "They can't touch what's mine."

My lips part in shock at his possessiveness, my body tensing, the anticipation growing.

Suddenly his mouth is on mine. He kisses me cruelly, almost painfully, his tongue choking me, his hips grinding into me. My purse hits the crushed stone of the driveway. My brain takes a second to catch up, even though my body is perfectly aware of what's happening. My nipples tingle, my core going tight as his other hand goes behind my head, holding me in place. I couldn't get out of his grip if I wanted to. Maybe that's why I kiss him back.

Or maybe it's just the lust I can't fight a second longer.

A lush ache commands me to press my hips into his, seeking some relief from the discomfort between my legs. The wind is even fiercer now, driving the cold, stinging rain over us both—but the lingering warmth of the Jag's engine and the heat of Dante's body on top of me make me burn. He pushes his hips insistently against me, pressing me against the hood of the car, the feel of his hard length drawing a harsh breath out of me. This is all happening so fast. My mind spins as if I'm drunk.

Every single touch makes it worse, like shots of tequila going straight to my inhibitions and breaking them down one by one. I hate him. Gone. I despise him.

Gone. I'm going to fight what his touch does to me. Gone, gone, gone.

He pulls back, shoving my skirt up so it bunches around my waist, taking me off guard a second time. I can't help but spread my legs wide as he grinds against me again, even though I'm battling my body's urges, desperately trying to resist what I know is coming: I'm going to give in to him and love every second of it. My body is going to betray me just like it did on my wedding night, heedless of the fact that Dante was using me solely for his own pleasure as I came again and again around his cock.

He takes his hand off my throat and thrusts it down the front of my underwear, crudely palming my mound, his fingers digging into my sensitive flesh. I push against him to suss out more of the delicious sensations coursing through me, a moan escaping my throat. It seems to flame him on. Dante streaks his fingers over my center, dragging his fingertips along my seam, and then he cups me again, hard. Bruising.

I take a full breath of air right before he rips my underwear down. The elastic cuts into the sides of my thighs, sticking to my wet skin, and then the fabric gives way in his impatient hand. My pussy is bared to him now, wet and ready and waiting. Meanwhile the sun has deserted us, leaving behind a shaded gloom. The sound of his zipper is muted against the wind, but it's unmistakable what he's doing.

His cock is out, hard and proud as he shoves my right leg up around his hip, driving into me with one possessive thrust. I cry out, my head lolling back as he wraps my other leg around him. Then he gets straight to work, fucking me hard and deep, the entire car bouncing with the force of his jackhammering. I cling to him, letting him ride me. My fingers clenched in his hair, my eyes shut against the falling rain.

Another storm begins to build, this one inside of me. Each thrust pushes me closer, somehow rubbing me just right, to the point where I'm hardly aware of the raindrops running into my hairline and clinging to my lashes. I can't stop my moans, coming faster and louder now as his hips pound into my inner thighs, his cock filling me, claiming me.

Possessing me.

I come right as a crack of thunder rips overhead. I barely hear it, I'm so consumed by the sensation of the orgasm taking over my entire body. My scalp tingles, my pulse rushes with the pleasure, stars shoot behind my clenched lids...it's so strong that Dante's release doesn't even register with me. I only know he's done because I realize that I'm suddenly very, very cold.

Sitting up, I see that Dante has zipped up and moved away. I wipe the rain from my eyes and try to gather myself as violent chills assail my body. I'm shaking so badly that I'm not sure my legs will support me if I try to stand up off the car. My knees feel like jelly, my arms weak.

Dante takes off his soaked suit jacket and comes over to me, wrapping it around my shoulders as he helps me up. The lining inside is mostly dry, the warmth and masculine scent of it enveloping me. I tug my skirt back down and pick my purse up off the driveway, touched and a little surprised by his kind gesture.

Who would have thought my husband had a single tender nerve in him to actually extend some chivalry like this? Especially to me, the wife he claims as nothing more than property.

Just then, a light shines from his cell phone, aimed at the car. He leans over, ignoring me, running his hand over the hood where we just fucked. The warmth in my chest dissipates as I realize he's checking for any dents we may have left behind. He hadn't been concerned about me one bit.

Hugging myself, the jacket's too-long sleeves hanging past my fingertips, I stomp my way around the side of the house as best I can in my new heeled sandals. Water runs down the back of my neck, my clothes clinging to my body inside the jacket. The wetness running down my legs gets worse as I reach the door. I'm acutely aware that it's definitely not from the rain.

I might laugh at the whole situation if I wasn't so infuriated.

What an asshole.

13

FRANKIE

I TAKE great delight in slamming the front door behind me just as Dante is reaching the top step of the porch. My moment of glee doesn't last long, though.

He pulls the door back open so hard, it bounces against the stop. Then he steps inside and closes it, dripping onto the marble floor. His eyes sweep over me and I brace for more of his scathing insults as I attempt to slip out of his soaked jacket. The sleeves cling to my arms, refusing to let go. He grins at my struggle, but there's no humor in it. He's merely mocking the difficult time I'm having.

After watching the show for another moment, he snags the sleeve and yanks, freeing one arm so I can wiggle out of the jacket completely.

"You could have used the back door. It would have been a shorter walk. Or maybe the domestic staff's door. Much more fitting."

Wadding up the sodden jacket, I fling it at him.

"Maybe I would have, if I actually knew there was a fucking back door to this mausoleum. But thanks for the suggestion anyway."

I take off my heels so I don't slip and stomp up the staircase that leads to my rooms. His footsteps follow me up, so I increase my pace. Darting over the threshold, I move to close my door as quickly as I can, but he's right behind me. I spin to face him as he barges inside, the look on his face making it clear he won't be denied.

My adrenaline kicks, another ache starting between my legs.

Dante kicks the door closed and advances on me. A shallow gasp leaves my throat as he grabs the lapel of my blazer and pulls me toward him.

I stumble from the momentum and fall into him, one hand on his chest. His warmth radiates through his damp shirt like the assault on my willpower that it is. Just this simple touch makes me want him. It's a hate-want. I hate that I want it. I don't want to want him, and this has to stop. A flush of embarrassment warms my cheeks at a quick memory of him thrusting into me against the car. He was uncaring, unfeeling, and yet it didn't bother me one bit.

His hands are suddenly everywhere, and my purse hits the floor, spilling its contents across the marble. He strips off my blazer and my blouse first, then unclasps my bra. I pull back, but the straps hold me in place, and then slide down my arms, the cups pulling free of my breasts and leaving them bare to his gaze.

Dante clenches his jaw and homes in on my nipples

as they harden almost painfully against the sudden exposure.

"What are you doing?" I'm almost yelling. "You must be fucking stupid if you think I'm going to let you fuck me again after that!"

My rage gives him pause, but it doesn't last as that cocky, irritating smirk claims his lips again. "I'd rather stick my dick into a beehive than back into a shrew bitch like you."

With a light shove, he strides over to the bathroom, where he grabs something behind the door. Crossing my arms over my chest, I barely have time to react as he launches a bathrobe at me the same way I'd thrown his coat at him. I scramble into it, pulling the tie much too tightly around my waist.

He disappears into the bathroom again and comes back with a towel. This time I'm prepared when he tosses it. "Dry your fucking hair. You look like a wet dog."

My jaw drops. "Well you look like a wet rat! And it has nothing to do with the rain."

Not my best comeback, but it will have to do.

He looks sharply past me and I follow his gaze over to the bed. It's piled high with a mound of shopping bags and boxes, all the purchases I made today. How the hell did those get in here? Donovan must have put them there when he got back earlier. Or wait, does this place have some kind of butler? I've seen plenty of staff around the house.

Dante makes a disgusted sound and storms from the room before I can ask. Blotting my hair with the towel, I find myself following him. I'm not done. Hell, I haven't even started.

"Excuse me, but we are not done here."

He doesn't break his stride. "Yes, we are."

"*Dante.*"

He continues down the hall, uncaring one bit that I'm on his heels.

"We need some ground rules," I insist. "I did not consent to what just happened again."

That's enough to stop him dead in his tracks, and he turns to face me, looking incredulous. Anger creeps up my neck to my face and makes my hairline tingle.

"Are you implying that I raped you?"

I falter, because my brain and my emotions are tumbling over each other. I don't like his cold, callous fucking. How easily he just takes what he wants while I don't even attempt to shut it down. What does that say about me?

"No," I blurt. "But it wasn't...I was..."

Dante waves me off as he throws open a door, revealing another lavish bedroom that I assume must be his. "I don't have time for this. I have to get to an important meeting."

I trail after him into the room. "We need to talk about what happened."

He ignores me and begins to whip off his wet clothes, shrugging out of his shirt and unfastening his pants. Each dusky inch of his body slowly revealed as the fabric disappears. He kicks free of his pants, standing there in his tight undies, the impressive outline of his cock visible through the damp fabric. I force myself to look past him, just so I can focus.

"I'm meeting Jessica in ten minutes," he says flatly. "Just go."

Right. He has an "important meeting." With Jessica. My ass.

He's watching me, waiting for me to react to his comment about her. But I bypass that for now. It's a fight for another day.

I try again. "I need to know that you're going to respect my boundaries, Dante."

"Did you ever once say no? Did a single word come out of your mouth to tell me you didn't want me, Francesca?"

My nostrils flare, my fingers clench. "Moving forward—"

He steps into his huge walk-in, not even listening. I focus on my breathing instead of berating him because honestly, I'm not sure where I'm even going with this conversation. I'm angry at myself for loving how he controls my body and the boundaries are more for me than him. The sounds of him dressing command my attention, almost making me forget what I was going to say. Why is this man so damn distracting?

He comes back out, fastening his cufflinks, long fingers working the link, twisting the backing, and pulling the sleeve. His button-down is light blue, a perfect complement to his dark coloring, the collar neatly buttoned at the tips, the top undone enough to reveal he's not wearing an undershirt beneath. Threads of dark, curling hair peek from the undone buttons as he makes a slight turn, the fabric pulling hard against his muscular torso. I give myself a mental shake.

Does he have to look so damned put together after fucking in the rain?

"Moving forward, what? You want me to keep my hands off you? Forget it. You're my wife."

I cross my arms. "That may be, but I insist that we come to some terms."

"You're ridiculous."

"I am not. This is my body and—"

He juts a hand at me palm out, silencing my tirade. Then he makes a move with his fingers as if I'm supposed to give him something. I have no idea what he wants.

"What?"

"The fucking credit card," he says impatiently. "And the keys to my new car. Now."

My heart is racing so fast, I can barely breathe. Fuming and feeling like I might burst from my anger, I spin around and head down the hall to my room, grabbing what he wants and then storming back. But instead of handing over the card and the keys like a good little Stepford wife, I march straight past him, throw open the French doors leading to his balcony, and step out into the storm. My eyes catch his and hang on as I launch the keys and the card as hard as I can over the railing and out into the rain.

I give a cocky jaunt of my head as I come back in and yank the balcony door closed, letting it slam satisfyingly behind me. I'm soaking wet again but oh wow, do I not give a *fuck*.

He follows me as I exit his room, with a hissed, "Jesus Christ" racing from his lips. I skirt past the staircase, Dante still on my heels as an overly sweet voice calls up to him.

"Dante, are you ready? We're going to be late."

Fucking Jessica.

"I'll be right down." Dante barks the words while staring at me.

It's my turn to smirk. I'll never let him see how much it pisses me off that she's literally at the bottom of the steps waiting for my husband to come to her.

"Go on, then," I say, doing my best impression of Jessica. "Let her suck the taste of me right off your dick."

I don't wait for a response as I go into my room, shut and lock the door, and then stand there until my pulse and my emotions wind down. I can hear his footfalls across the marble floor, descending the steps, and then fading completely. Good riddance.

I imagine Jessica waiting downstairs with open arms, her boobs nearly popping out of whatever she's wearing. With a huff that's so unlike me, I go to the bathroom and fill the tub with water as hot as I can stand. Then I add a generous pour from a bottle of Lollia bubble bath, inhaling deeply as the scent of white tea and honeysuckle fills the room. I need to soak both the chill and the touch of my husband out of me.

The water stings as I sink into it, but I grit my teeth and wait it out as my skin adjusts and the burn becomes welcome relief. But as I close my eyes and enjoy the tickle of bubbles against my jaw, I somehow can't stop thinking about Dante.

His eyes had been so determined, so intense as he'd ripped my panties off me. My fingers stray down there, exploring my hips, my thighs. I didn't look, but I'm sure there are marks from the force of the elastic digging into my skin. I remember the feel of his palm against me, pressing, his fingers stroking and searching until I was helpless with want.

A flood of desire washes over me. Closing my eyes, I let my fingers wander to the ache, plunging them inside me, recreating the sensation Dante had caused when he'd fucked me against the car. I spread my legs and stretch out in the oversized tub. He'd kissed me so hard. I never realized that kind of aggression was something I'd enjoy.

I slip my fingers out and rub my palm over my center, feeling my own wetness as I thumb my clit and start making slow little circles around it. I wish he'd kissed my neck, my breasts. Maybe worked his way lower until that wicked tongue was right here where my fingers are. Tension swirls and cascades as I rub and stroke, trying to get some relief. But the more I try not to think about Dante, the more I flash back to his granite face, the naked desire in his dark eyes, the hard perfection of that proud cock.

And the more I imagine him, the closer I get. It was foolish to think I could set boundaries on whatever this is between us. I want it, even though it's so far from something I ever imagined I would enjoy. It's as if I've become a different person in the few short days I've been Dante's wife.

A swirl of sweet tension flies high, bringing me to the edge, and I start panting with anticipation, my free hand sliding up to squeeze my breast. But no matter how hard I try, how close I get, I can't seem to get there. Even when I reimagine the rough sex against the car, it's no use. I can't reach the place I'm looking for. My release escapes me.

14

FRANKIE

Hello, new wardrobe.

I turn from side to side before my full-length mirror, assessing the outfit I've chosen to wear to dinner tonight. I've dressed well, every stitch of clothing brand new and very expensive. I know I look my best, too, in a vivid red dress that covers me from neck to knee. A strip cutout over my chest shows off a few inches of tantalizing skin, but it's a subtle tease—nothing too flashy.

It's absolutely perfect. There's not a thing about it that Dante can scoff at or complain about. Then again, from what I know of him so far, he'll find something to nitpick.

Slipping into my heels, I can't help wondering what time he arrived home after his "meeting" with Jessica last night. I fell asleep shortly after my bath, despite my determination to wait up and listen for his footsteps in the hall. Who knows? Maybe he was out all night. Asshole.

Double-checking my makeup one last time, I finally make my way down to the dining room. I'm ten minutes late, on purpose, partly because I'm nervous about seeing my husband again after our face-off last night, and partly because I want to make him wait. Antagonizing him comes pretty naturally, and I can't deny there's a part of me that likes getting a reaction out of him. He certainly knows how to drum one out of me, so fair is fair.

Dante and Armani are already seated when I walk into the room. There are fresh flowers on the table, carafes of what must be Bellanti wines, baskets of steaming crostini and garlic focaccia, and a few small plates of caponata and olive oil and balsamic vinegar sprinkled with dry herbs. I'm drooling at the spread, and these are only the appetizers. Whatever's currently underway in the kitchen, it also smells incredible.

My heart flutters as Dante's eyes sweep over me. He boldly tracks me as I move to the place setting across from him. I'm not sure if that setting is for me or Marco, but the youngest Bellanti brother is never on time—so I'm claiming it. I want to see my husband head-on, not from the side. It's time I learn to read him a little better, and for that, I need an unobstructed view of his mannerisms. He doesn't correct my choice of seats.

As I pour myself some wine to match the full glasses of my companions, I notice my husband's dark hair is perfectly swept back, the way his powerful shoulders look in the tailored cut of his jacket. It drums up memories of the strength of his arms holding me in place against the Jag in the rain, how I'd clung to him. He looks away, scowling as if annoyed, and turns his attention to his phone.

Armani shoots him an eyebrow, then leans his forearms on the table and gives me a warm smile. "That is an amazing dress, Francesca. You look lovely."

Armani is far and away my favorite Bellanti. "Thank you. That's nice of you to say."

Just then, Marco strides in and says, "Watch yourself, brother. *I'm* supposed to be the smooth one."

I turn in my chair and do a double take. He's got a woman on each arm, both of them in tight bodycon dresses, with matching high ponytails and quite a bit of makeup. He winks at me. "I'm going to need another arm just for you. And if you don't mind me saying so, you look *much* too good to be sitting across from that grumpy old man."

The women with him smile stiffly, but I burst out laughing. "Thank you, Marco."

When I turn back around, I see Dante glaring at me. I just smile wider.

Marco strolls over to Armani and claps him on the shoulder. "And you need to work on upping your compliment game if you're ever going to win over Candi."

"No idea what you're talking about," Armani says, but I catch the glint in his eye.

I perk up at this little tidbit of gossip. Armani and Candi?

Expecting Marco to announce that the three of them are skipping dinner for the club, I'm surprised when he maneuvers his dates toward the table and gestures for them to sit.

Dante's voice makes everyone go still. "This is a *family* dinner, Marco."

He pointedly eyes the female duo that Marco just seated while wearing that intimidating, expressionless mask that I've come to know. It might not show anything, but it doesn't mean he's not going to blow at any moment. Don't I know all too well how that side of him works.

Marco hitches a brow, a guarded, cocky expression working over his face. He juts his chin out at me. "*She's* here."

I sit up a little straighter. My interactions with Marco thus far have been limited, and I don't know him well at all. His attempt to drag me into his argument with Dante isn't cool.

"*She* is my wife," Dante growls possessively.

Tingles shoot through me when he calls me that, at the way he's claimed me with just one word—and in front of his brothers, too.

Marco just leans back in his chair, spreading his hands with an unperturbed grin. "Right. Your wife. Hell, after what these two just did for me, I'm probably going to marry them, too."

Dante slams a fist on the table. The flatware vibrates against the china, my wine rippling in my glass. Swallowing hard, I swing my gaze to Dante. Tension rolls off him, palpable and stirring. There's not a trace of impassivity left and my middle clenches. I don't think I've even seen half the anger my husband is capable of. Nor do I want to.

Before he can reply, I clear my throat and smile.

"You know," I say easily, turning to Armani. "I've actually known Candi for quite a while—we went to high school together. She's a great person."

There's a flicker of something in Armani's eyes, but I can't quite tell what it is. I'm sure it's obvious to him (and everyone else) that I'm trying to break up the fight.

Marco smirks and begins speaking to Dante in Italian, his tone hard and sarcastic. Apparently he's unaware that I can understand every single word.

"Your new wife seems to be well trained," he says.

Dante takes a leisurely sip of his wine, as if he's got all day to respond. Or perhaps he's considering if it's worth his time to engage in this fight.

"You're a reckless asshole, fratellino," he shoots back in Italian, referring to Marco as 'little brother,' though his tone makes it sound more like an insult than a term of endearment. *"One who neglects the family business in favor of fucking your way through the Bay Area and engaging in drunken fights that reflect poorly on us all. Sei un imbarazzo."*

That last comment has me looking down into my wineglass, wishing I really didn't understand what they were saying. Dante just told Marco he's an embarrassment.

Armani glances between his brothers but remains silent. His shoulders set hard, a little muscle bouncing in his jaw. I get the impression he's used to sitting back while these two play out their irritations with each other. He doesn't seem in a hurry to interrupt, but I get the feeling that he's fully prepared to step up if the need arises.

Marco scoffs. *"At least I know how to fuck a woman properly.* Your *wife is clearly unsatisfied, seeing as how you don't even share a bedroom. Maybe I should give you some lessons, eh? Let you borrow my friends here for a few practice rounds?"*

He wiggles his brows, and Dante's whole body goes taut as he shoots back, *"You need to watch where you stick your dick, Marco. The Brunos have eyes everywhere."*

Tension ratchets in the room and I find myself mindlessly pulling at the hem of my dress. Maybe being ten minutes late wasn't the wisest choice. I should have waited longer, like...never. I could have had a greasy burger and fries delivered to my room and spent the evening watching Schitt's Creek. I really didn't need this tonight, not after all of last night's drama.

"That's funny, brother," Marco says. *"You're one to tell me to be careful who I fuck."*

The inflections in their words and force of their tones suggest they're seconds away from an all-out yelling match, or possibly a physical altercation. I shift uncomfortably in my seat, eyes flicking toward the door. That's when I notice Armani watching me, so I try to look confused, pretending not to understand what's going on.

Fuck you guys, I think. *I'm fucking fluent.* I spent three years speaking nothing but Italian every single day, so joke's on them. And there are more than a few things I could say right back, but of course I won't. Let them fight. I don't have a stake in this argument, and I'd rather play my cards close to the vest. The Bellantis not knowing I speak Italian could come in handy later.

The kitchen door swings open, and two men in aprons come out with the salad course.

Dante cools his features back into his trademark impassive face. Marco's apparently had enough, though, because he gets out of his chair before the food is set down and ushers his dates toward the door, switching back to English as he herds them out.

"Sincerest apologies for my brother's rude behavior, ladies," he says loudly. "Let's go out tonight instead of sitting in this viper's nest. You've both earned it."

He makes a show of pinching them each on the ass on their way out.

Without acknowledging anything going on in the dining room, the waitstaff set the plates down and then fill our glasses, then leave as if nothing out of the ordinary has taken place. Maybe it hasn't. Maybe this is just par for the course at Casa Bellanti.

Armani stares at his salad with a blank look. There are shadows beneath his eyes and a furrow in his brow. He looks tired. Probably exhausted by his family, and from what little I've experienced so far, it seems like it doesn't take much for this group to wear each other down with their bickering. He smooths his tie as he stands and nods politely at me, then Dante.

My husband speaks in English as he picks up his wineglass. "Where the hell do you think you're going?"

"If you'll excuse me, I'm not very hungry. And I've got a morning meeting to prep for."

"Armani," Dante says.

Armani gives a slight bow. "Good night, brother. Francesca."

Then he's gone, leaving me and Dante alone, and we haven't even gotten past the salad course yet.

Meeting, my ass. *Why couldn't you take me with you?* I scream in my mind. Picking up my wineglass, I swirl it gently and eye my husband over the rim as I sip. It's a sweet red but the delicious notes do little to temper the bitterness of my words.

Raising a finger, I tick off each word aimed at Dante. "Criminals, senators, mobsters, princes. I didn't see any elected officials or royalty here tonight, so what does that make your brothers?"

I take another sip of wine.

Dante doesn't answer.

15

FRANKIE

"I'D LIKE to go to my father's house, please. You can just drop me off, and I'll call when I'm ready to leave."

Donovan opens the car door for me. "Apologies, Mrs. Bellanti," he says kindly, if a little uncomfortably. "I'm not allowed to leave you anywhere."

I go still, reluctant to get into the back seat now. "You don't have to wait for me. Really. I might be there all day, and it's only a few minutes from here."

He smiles in that practiced, yet genuinely warm way. "I'm happy to wait as long as it takes, Mrs. Bellanti. It *is* my job."

"But—" I pull in a breath. I know this isn't his fault, but I can't help feeling pissed about it. A little sick over the whole thing, actually. My husband has apparently forbidden me to go anywhere—even right here in town, to see my own fucking family—without a chaperone.

"I'm sorry, ma'am," Donovan repeats. "Would you like to revise your itinerary?"

With a sigh, I tell him no, and that I understand. "And I appreciate that you're looking out for me," I add, slipping into the back seat. He seems relieved that I'm not kicking up a fuss.

But the whole drive to the Abbott compound, I feel the invisible chains around me. Isn't the joke supposed to be that the husband wears the ball and chain? Because I'm finding that to be completely ass backwards in my case. Dante has made me his prisoner. I hate it.

I was already tense about visiting my homestead today. Seeing Livvie is my purpose, but I'm still uncertain about how I'll feel if I run into our father. I haven't forgiven him by a long shot for forcing me into this marriage. So far, nothing good has come out of it for me except a couple unexpectedly hot orgasms and a shopping spree—both of which I certainly didn't need a marriage certificate to obtain.

The grounds are quiet as we arrive. The lawn appears recently mown and the flowerbeds lining the house are neatly planted and weeded. Curious about the landscape refresh, I enter the house to find Livvie and immediately notice that a few of Charlie's paintings have been professionally framed and hung in the entry hall. The living room sports new, expensive-looking furniture and the hardwood floors are polished and gleaming. The house looks remarkably clean.

"Hey, Frankie."

My father walks down the hall toward me, a beer in his hand. He's actually smiling. I return the smile hesitantly because I'm very confused about all the sudden changes around here.

"Looking good in here, Dad. New furniture?"

He takes a swig from his bottle. I wince, wishing I could tear it from his hand.

"You should take a look around the vineyard. The winery is doing better than ever under your new husband. Things have really started to turn around for us."

My jaw clenches. It's been, like, a few days since the wedding. There's no way in hell the winery could have turned around so fast—Dad's clearly lying. A little window dressing can't change the fact that the vines will need years to fully bounce back, that the tasting room needs to be completely overhauled, that the Abbott name and reputation have been sullied all over Napa.

But no matter. I'm not here for him.

"That's great, Dad. I guess my arranged marriage is really working out for you. Congratulations. Now where's Livvie?" I demand, less than politely.

His eyes grow a little cold. "Your sister's in the barn. She could probably use your help with her chores."

Just like that, I'm reduced from the adult woman who apparently saved his ass to the teenager trapped under his thumb. He walks away, the sound of his boots loud on the floor. A minute later, the door to his office shuts and I'm certain I hear a faint click of the lock. I wonder what he's hiding behind that closed door.

I go to the mudroom, hang up my purse, and slip out of my shoes. My old riding boots are neatly lined up on the rubber tray, just like old times. Nostalgia pangs through me as I sit down to put them on. The shafts are a bit stiff, but my feet easily slide into them. They're familiar and comfortable and remind me of when my sisters and I used to race each other to see who could get their boots on first before heading out to do chores—last one done had to muck out the stalls. I'd really missed the camaraderie while I was in Italy.

Walking the cobbled path to the barn, I hear Livvie's voice from the run-down round pen out back. I find her there working with a large black horse on a lead, circling her in a high-stepped trot. Our family has bred Friesian horses for as long as I can remember. They're gorgeous and agile, wonderful for both riding and light farmwork. At one point, our herd was yet another asset to the Abbott name—one that slowly began dwindling long before I'd gone to Italy. I'm almost afraid to look in the barn and see what's left.

Livvie doesn't notice me and I don't want to disturb her, so I lean my arms on the fence and just enjoy the sun and the sight of my sister doing something she loves. She's always had an easy, natural way with horses, and they respond to her much differently than they do to me or Charlie or our dad. While we all loved to ride growing up, Charlie and I never had the ingrained passion for all things horse that Livvie does. She's so at ease right now, so focused. I envy the peacefulness on her face, her stance, and as I watch I'm reminded once again how glad I am to have taken a bullet for her by marrying Dante.

Even if it is fucking miserable.

She redirects the horse into a slow canter, a gait that isn't easy for this particular breed. But the gelding glides into it with a graceful rebound step that makes him look like a rocking horse. Finally, she orders him to a walk, and when he stops he turns to face her. She notices me then and waves eagerly. The horse tosses his head, his impressively long black mane billowing with the movement.

"Did you come to ride with me? That's where I'm headed next!"

Smiling, I say, "I didn't, but I will—even though I'm rusty. It should be lots of fun seeing me on a horse again."

"You'll be fine," Livvie says. "It's like riding a bicycle."

"Not for me it isn't," I tell her with a laugh. "This is going to be a challenge."

Not to mention painful. I haven't ridden in three years, and going that long without means that my legs, ass, and thighs will be aching tomorrow. You don't realize how many muscles you use to ride a horse until you don't do it for a while.

I open the gate for her and she brings the horse through. I pet his nose.

"Who is this?" I ask. "I don't recognize his face. Is he new?"

"He's sort of new. He's a four-year-old. Dad bought him right after you left for Italy. He needs to go through some more dressage training, but he's had enough that I can start showing him. Well, maybe."

Her voice trails off sadly. There's clearly more to that

story, but I don't prod. We reach the side barn doors and Livvie puts her hand over mine on the door handle.

"Wait. It's, um, not the same as when you left. I've been trying to keep up, but I'm not really handy when things break and there's only so much maintenance I know how to do. Plus, almost all of the horses are gone." My stomach drops. Livvie smiles, looking suddenly perky though the shadow of sadness is clear in her eyes. "But don't worry, Ytse is still here. I tied him in the woods out back when the buyer was here. Dad forgot about him, and never said a word when he mysteriously reappeared in his stall."

"Oh, Livvie." I squeeze her hand. "I'm so sorry. Thank you."

I imagine her leading my gelding Ytse into the woods in the dark of morning and waiting it out as the horse buyer made a sweep of our barns, then skirting him back in when the coast was clear. Our father was probably too drunk to notice. I grew up riding Ytse. He's old now, and I can't explain how it feels to know my sister preserved him for me.

"He'll be happy to see you," she says.

She opens the doors and leads her horse in. I follow, pausing in the aisle to take it all in. Livvie wasn't kidding. These barns were once stately, in perfect condition. Like the horses, this building had been a jewel in the Abbott crown. Now it's all sagging and hanging boards, broken gates, exposed wires, and cobwebs.

Livvie hoses off the horse's legs, gives him a quick

rubdown, and then puts him in his stall. It's perfectly clean, a new rubber mat peeking from the fresh bedding. All the stalls on this side are the same. Tidy, cared for. But the opposite side and other aisle are in complete disrepair. We once housed twenty-two prized Friesians in here. Now it's barely livable for the few left.

Just then, a long, shaggy black head pops over a stall door as a horse nickers at me.

"Ytse!" I coo, going over to him to rub his nose. "Hi, baby. How's my sweet boy?"

"Come change your clothes," Livvie's voice calls from the tack room.

Pulling away from my sweet old gelding, I go to the tack room and find it completely spotless. Saddles, bridles, halters, and gear hang in perfect order on the walls. Livvie holds up my old riding pants and a sweater. We each kept a tote of riding clothes in the barn so we could change on a whim and go riding. It's a good thing, too, because I'm not sure my skinny jeans and silk top are appropriate for the trail. I grab my tote and head into the restroom to see if I can still fit into my jodhpurs. They're a little tight, but I manage.

Livvie changed in the tack room and is already getting Ytse ready for me when I come out. He paws at straw in the aisle but stands quietly for his saddle. My sister is so in her element that I let her tack him up instead of stepping in, and soon we're mounted and heading down a familiar trail through the back of the property.

The sun is warm, birds are singing, and soft clouds

roll across the sky. I could almost forget what my life has turned into and forget that I'm not Frankie Abbott anymore. The one who used to do this with her sisters nearly every day.

Livvie half swivels in the saddle to look back at me. Her horse is antsy and prancing sideways as if ready to run, but she's making it easy on me by holding him back and keeping our pace to a slow amble. She knows full well I won't be able to keep up with my tender ass.

"Let's ride to Delores's for fruit cups. Just like old times."

"Sounds good!"

We make our way through the vines and take the winding trail to the Alvarez property to visit with Delores while we have a snack and let the horses rest. Afternoon is well upon us by the time we leave and have a leisurely ride back. Livvie is nonstop chatter about the horses, her senior year of high school, cute boys, and the colleges she's been looking into.

When she finally stops talking to come up for air, I take the opportunity to casually bring up her new horse. "You were saying something earlier about showing him in dressage. Isn't the yearly pre-qualifier coming up?"

Charlie and Livvie showed their horses religiously in the state pre-qualifiers and then worked their way into bigger events. Me? I just went for the snacks.

Livvie kicks her feet from the stirrups and lets them hang, swinging them gently back and forth. "Yeah, it is, but I won't be going."

"Too busy?" I prod teasingly. "I didn't know you had such a robust social life now."

"Ha ha."

Her entire countenance changes and an uneasy feeling creeps up on me. "Come on, Liv. Tell me what's going on."

I nudge my horse to catch up with hers and pull up so we're side by side. She shrugs and looks straight ahead. "Dad sold the truck and trailer a few months ago, so I wouldn't be able to get there. But even if he hadn't, I... can't really afford the entry fee this year."

My heart sinks at the realization that my baby sister has been left to bear the brunt of our father's mistakes ever since Charlie and I left home. Guilt claws at me.

"Livvie, I am so sorry that I haven't been around."

We're back at the barn now and she dismounts gracefully. "Don't be. You left to help the family. And I'm happy for you. Besides, I can take care of myself. And Charlie always helps out when things get really bad."

"Good. But now that I'm back, you can come to me, too. I'm always here for you."

Once I'm off my horse, I pull her in for a hug, silently vowing to make my father pay for his mistakes. I leave Livvie to her work (there's always more work for her to do, it seems) and head back to the house. I'd be happy to help her, but the sun is starting to sink and I want to be home before dinner so I don't ruffle Dante's feathers. He left a brand-new cell phone by my coffee cup this morning and I'm surprised he hasn't called a hundred times already.

In the mudroom, I pull off my boots, only to find that one of my socks is damp and muddy. Inspecting my boot, I find the leather around the bottom of the heel is starting to separate from the sole. Lovely. And now my sock is too gross to put my tennis shoes back on. Barefoot, I pad down the hall to Livvie's room to borrow a fresh pair of socks. I know she won't mind.

En route, I overhear my father's voice filtering from behind his office door. The sound of his raw, harsh laughter stops me in my tracks. What the hell is he so jolly about?

"Sure thing, Phil," he's saying. "Just put me down for five grand on number two-one-two. Yeah...perfect. And five hundred on one-one-eight."

I can't believe it. That motherfucker is still gambling. He lost it all, from the family vineyard to his own flesh and blood, and yet he's learned nothing. Blood boiling, I'm about to bust my way in and confront him with a few choice words when—

"Bellanti? Yeah, why? You need a car tampered with, too? Ha! ...sure, I know the guy. I can recommend his services. But it's gonna cost you."

Bellanti? A car? He's talking about Dante's father.

His death wasn't an accident.

My scalp tingles, my muscles freezing even as something inside screams at me to get out before my father finds me eavesdropping here in the hallway. Covering my mouth with my hand, I tiptoe back the way I came. Screw the socks.

Heart pounding, almost dizzy with adrenaline and

the force of my pulse, I carry my shoes out to the waiting car, still barefoot, barely aware of Donovan opening the door for me as I slip into the back seat and try not to vomit.

Enzo Bellanti was murdered.

And my father was somehow involved.

FRANKIE

THE PARKING LOT at Bella Notte is full when we arrive. Donovan circles the lot a few times and then tells me he'll park in the fire lane so he can keep an eye on the restaurant while I'm in there. Apparently the possibility of a parking ticket isn't any kind of threat to the Bellantis' driver.

I called Charlie on the way over to ask her to meet me here for dinner. I have no idea what to do with the information I just stumbled onto, but there's no way I can carry this alone. My father is a...a what?

A murderer? An accessory to murder? A criminal mastermind?

I can't prove any of that, of course, or even ascertain that he was directly involved in Enzo Bellanti's death. But he did spill that the accident wasn't an accident at all, and he claims to know who arranged the fatal details. Someone in my father's close circle dirtied their hands to

145

kill a man. Fear razors down my spine and I'm not sure I can get out of the car.

"Sorry for keeping you out all day." I stumble over the words as Donovan comes around to open the rear door for me. He frowns at the distress I'm doing a shitty job at hiding.

"I'm happy to be of service, Mrs. Bellanti."

"I'll, um, just have a quick bite with my sister and—"

"Madam, please." He lightly touches my wrist. "Take all the time you'd like, and enjoy your evening. It's no trouble at all."

Glancing into his kind eyes, I nod. "Thanks, Donovan."

I wonder what he's seen, what he's heard in his time with the Bellantis. It would probably make the information I'm carrying look like child's play. What's worse? Being exposed to such heinous behavior for the first time, or being exposed so often that you finally become immune?

I'll never let myself become that person. Charlie's husband is involved in things she knows enough to stay out of, but even so, I hope the exposure by proxy doesn't harden her to these things, either. We simply cannot turn out like our father.

Once I'm inside, I remember I'm not really dressed for this place in my jeans and blouse, my sneakers and no socks. But the hostess gives me the most welcoming smile anyway, as if I'm dressed to the nines *and* have a reservation.

"Mrs. Bellanti! How very nice to see you again."

I can't place her beaming face, so if we've met, I have no recollection of it. She seems to know me, though. "Um, thank you."

"May I offer you a table this evening?" she asks.

"Actually, yes. I need a private booth. Sorry I didn't call ahead."

She scrunches her nose in a cute little way. "You never need to call, Mrs. Bellanti. Your family's table is always available to you."

Family table? Okay. I guess it's just another perk of being a Bellanti. Who am I to argue? Especially when I need to sit down and have a damn drink. I follow the woman to the back, but don't get far before a couple I don't recognize calls out to me.

"Nice to see you this evening, Mrs. Bellanti."

"Such a pretty blouse!"

I smile and nod, walk a couple feet, and get stopped again. I recognize this couple, at least. They were the ones who scowled and turned their noses up at me when I met Dante here. I'm receiving a much warmer reception now, however.

"Oh, Francesca. Marriage is looking good on you!" the woman simpers.

"Please give your husband our regards," her husband adds. "The Hartwells."

Stunned by the about-face, I just nod again.

At this point, I'm aware that a lot of people in the dining area are staring at me, just like last time—but their attitudes are markedly different this go-round. Apparently being Dante's wife means I'm suddenly worth their time.

The hostess seats me and I order a bottle of rosé, along with two fingers of whiskey neat.

"And two place settings, please. I'll order now, too."

"Of course."

Without even consulting a menu, I order a carb fest of Italian comfort food classics: pasta carbonara, lasagna, fried ravioli, garlic knots, and two desserts, which I request to be brought out along with the meal—tiramisu and profiteroles. I need all the sugar and starch I can stand to help process what I'd overheard.

A waiter returns to pour the wine just as Charlie shows up and slides into the booth.

"Hey, you," she says, setting her purse on the seat and sipping her wine.

I'm so relieved to see her that tears sting my eyes. She takes one look at me and her forehead creases.

"What's wrong, Frankie?"

It's impossible to speak with how upset I am, so I drain half my glass first, clearing my throat after I set it down. "Before I get into all that, we need to talk about Livvie. One of us has to take her. She cannot stay home alone with Dad. Not anymore. So either I take her or you do."

"Okay, I'll talk it over with—"

"No. There's no time for that. Like, this has to happen tonight."

Charlie scoots closer and swallows hard. "What did he do?"

"You sure you really want to know?"

I polish off my wine and reach for the bottle for a refill. She puts her hand over mine.

"Listen," she says quietly. "My husband is off on some mysterious work trip for an 'indeterminate amount of time.' His words, not mine. But you know Livvie won't leave her horses longer than one night, so why don't I just move back into the house for now? That would be easier than running her back and forth every day."

My throat is dry, despite the wine. I nod. "Okay. For now."

"You're scaring me, Frankie. You weren't even this upset when you found out about your surprise wedding."

I give a humorless smile. "This is just a tad worse than that."

Our food shows up before I get a chance to elaborate. My sister sits back frowning as the waiters set down the dishes, top off our wine, grate us some fresh parmesan, and finally leave.

"Were you expecting someone else? Perhaps an entire army?" my sisters asks. "This is a lot of food."

Twirling spaghetti around my fork, I wave off her sarcasm. "Just shut up and eat."

Hesitantly, she picks up her fork and stabs a ravioli. I sample each of the dishes, but my heart's not really in it. Finally, Charlie sets her fork down with a clank and stares at me. I pause mid-bite. She gives me an eye roll when I gesture to her empty plate.

"That lasagna isn't going to eat itself."

"Frankie, come on. You've got me so worried about what's going on that I can't eat, okay? Whatever it is, just spill it."

"Okay, okay, I'm sorry." I wipe my mouth and grasp the stem of my wineglass. Glancing around first to make sure no one is listening in, I lower my voice to a whisper. "I overheard Dad talking to one of his bookies. He said that...that he knew the name of the person who tampered with Enzo Bellanti's car. It had to be what caused the accident that night, right?"

We lock eyes. Charlie's face goes white. "I don't know. Maybe Dad was just gossiping."

"No. He *recommended* the guy's 'services,' Char. What does that sound like to you?"

She lets out a breath, shaking her head. "Are you absolutely sure you heard what you think you did?"

"Yes!" The word snaps out of me. "I was standing right outside his office door. I heard every single word loud and clear."

"Okay, okay. I believe you. This is just a lot. I mean Dad is no angel, but...how involved is he in this?"

"No idea." I shrug and drink more wine, though my stomach is in knots and pretty close to rejecting everything I just ate.

"You're right. Liv shouldn't be alone with him. We'll figure something out."

"Here's another question. Should I tell Dante?"

Her brow furrows. "Of course you should. You're tied to him now."

Scowling, I whine, "But I hate him. Why should I help him?"

My sister tries to hide a tiny smile, which I know is her amusement over my brattiness. "I know you're having a hard time, but like it or not, you're a Bellanti. That means your loyalty is to them. Dante's successes are yours, too, and his failures...well, those are all his own.

"But the better he does, the better you—and all of us Abbotts—will do. And if Dad's involved in something shady, do you really think it's up to you to protect him from the consequences, Frankie? *I* wouldn't. He deserves whatever payback comes his way."

I have to admit, I've had the same thought. "Maybe you're right."

"I'm always right," she says.

She dips a garlic knot in marinara and then stuffs the entire thing into her mouth, shooting me a wink. We used to stress eat together. We called it bonding.

By the time we get to the desserts, we've shifted from brooding and stressed to overstuffed and stressed, but I'm somewhat relieved to have shared my burdens.

Pushing the tiramisu away, Charlie says, "Here's the thing. This information you have now? It's the leverage you were missing before. So use it."

"I'm not following," I say. "Use it for what?"

"To renegotiate the terms of your relationship with Dante," she says. "You want a financial cut of their winery? A job? Something to secure Livvie's future? This is how you're going to get it."

I mull her words over in my mind as I finish my

dessert and my wine, but something about all of this is still nagging me. "How does that make me any better than Dad? I'm trading information about someone's death for my personal gain."

I don't want to be that person.

"You are nothing like Dad," Charlie says. "Look at it this way. He's left nothing for Livvie. Nada. If you can get something out of this for her, then you've done a good thing."

Despite all the food, I suddenly feel deflated. "I don't know. I hate this."

My sister reaches over and takes my hand. "I know that it's not easy, Frankie. You didn't ask for any of this."

"Better me than Livvie, right?"

"Right. And you can bet your ass I'm going to do a lot of listening and probably a little snooping while I'm at Dad's house. Speaking of which, I should head out so I can pack a bag and get over there."

She opens her purse and takes out a credit card, but I stop her.

"I'm sure the Bellantis have a tab. Just get to Livvie. Love you guys."

"Love you too. Mwah."

I'm sad to see her go, but glad to know she'll be at Livvie's side for the time being. If our father has been up to this nonsense since we've been out of the house, what else has he done? He's put our whole family at risk.

My stomach churns.

I know the Bellantis are involved in underhanded

things—it's no secret that it's made them very rich. The whole reason I married Dante was to save my family from financial ruin.

But how far am I willing to go to protect what's mine?

I can't shake the feeling that I'm about to find out.

1 7

FRANKIE

I SENSE Dante as soon as I walk into the house.

It's been a long day. My thighs ache from horseback riding and I want nothing more than to slip into a hot bath, but I need to talk to my husband and make my confession.

I've already made up my mind that I'm going to tell him what I overheard, but I still don't know what I want in return. I'm not even sure how to hold information like this hostage. I'm hoping seeing his face will inspire something in me, good or bad. Either my inner gangster will come out, or I'll flake and crumble.

Slipping off my shoes, I pad down the darkened hall-way, toward the low light spilling from a doorway. I'm fairly certain it's one of the living rooms (not the one with the movie screen in it), but it could also be the library. Or the spare office. Or the games room with the pool table. Hell, who am I kidding? I can barely keep track of my own rooms in this place. Plus, I may have polished off Charlie's wine once she'd left—and the rest of the bottle—to help me work up the nerve to come home and face Dante. So I'm a little discombobulated, truth be told.

Regardless, it turns out my instincts are dead-on.

When I enter the living room, Dante is standing near the brick fireplace, looking out a window into the dark. His profile is to me. He's holding a glass of wine, his tie loose, the neckline of his shirt open. He's striking in the soft amber light. Then again, when isn't he?

If I could get away with it, I'd be content to simply stand here and watch him brood, but he intuits I'm here. Slowly, he turns to look at me, taking a small drink before settling his eyes on mine and hanging on there.

It strikes me how different we are. We're two very separate people.

But I'm about to step fully into his world, and when I'm done offloading what I know, I pray I'll be able to leap right back out.

"Bella Notte with your sister." He turns back to the window. "How was your meal?"

It's not a real question—more like words to fill the space. I'm hardly surprised that he knew where I was and with whom. He could have microchipped me in my sleep for all I know.

"Very good. As was the wine. I had almost a whole bottle to myself."

He looks at me again, nodding to himself. "My wife is a drunk."

"Maybe. I wasn't, up until a few days ago...when my

life took a drastic and unexpected turn. Can you blame me?"

I make my way over to him. He doesn't acknowledge my sarcasm, or my approach.

"Dante, look. We need to come to some kind of truce. Unfortunately, we're stuck with each other, and spending the rest of our lives fighting is just going to give us both ulcers."

He flicks me a look, filled with disdain. "A truce implies we reach a mutually beneficial agreement. What could I possibly want from you that would benefit me?"

I lean my hip against the side of the sofa. He's close enough that I could smack the haughty sneer off his lips if I were a braver, or more violent, person.

"My help," I suggest. "My expertise. My knowledge."

He scoffs, as if what I've just said is ludicrous, and I feel my face go hot.

"Do you even know why I spent the last three years in Italy?" I ask, losing patience.

It's a rhetorical question. Of course he doesn't. He never cared to ask.

He smiles at me over the rim of his glass. "Fucking your way through Sicily?"

I don't smile back. "If I were more like you, then yes, that is exactly what I would have been doing. Instead of fucking, however, I was earning my master's degree in soil sciences with a focus on enhancing vine production. My undergrad program at UC Berkeley was a double major in business marketing and agriscience. I've had a sommelier certification since I was twenty-two—"

"Bravo," Dante says dryly, but I don't let him goad me.

"I've been training to run a winery my *entire life*. My father, supremely lazy ass that he was, made sure I could do all his work for him someday. So, dear husband, you tell me. Does that sound beneficial to you?"

He tries to dismiss me with an off-putting laugh, but I don't accept it. Moving to him, I grab his glass out of his hand just as he moves to take a drink. I smell the alcohol, take a small sip, then a larger one.

"French brandy with a base of..." I close my eyes, mining the encyclopedic knowledge in my brain. "Let's see, the river Garonne, right bank...that makes it Saint-Émilion wine, Grand Cru of course, aged two years."

I open my eyes and find Dante paying attention now, though he's trying not to show it.

"The appellation specializes in red wines with a crisp, full finish," I go on, "and I'm getting very strong notes of plum and cherry—suggesting production from grapes grown in a temperate year. Hmm, I'm surprised. I'd think it a bit fruity for a man like you."

I finish off the rest of the glass and hand it back to him empty.

"Fill it with something else and let's make a game of it, shall we? I can do this all night."

One corner of his mouth turns up, but he quickly schools it. I've got him. I see the curiosity, the surprise in his eyes. So much for his poker face.

"I can be useful to you, Dante. I know things." Oh, hell, the alcohol is going straight to my mouth. "About your wines, about your grapes...about the unfortunate mealybug infestation in the southeast corner that's threatening your newest vines."

He's fully facing me, his body taut. I should stop talking. Instead I lean closer, nearly touching him.

"About the death of your father."

He grabs my shoulders, all pretense gone. "What do you know?"

This is it—and I'm not prepared. Despite Charlie's advice, I haven't figured out what to ask for in trade for this information. Letting out a breath, I realize it doesn't matter. I can't honestly use this as a bartering tool. It feels too wrong.

"It wasn't an accident. Somebody did something to his car. I overheard my dad talking on the phone about it. He offered to sell that person's name to whomever he was speaking with."

Dante is so still he might well be a statue. I don't know how I was expecting him to react when he found out, but it wasn't like this. Maybe he already suspected? Or is his granite face just hiding overwhelming anger, or disbelief? His nostrils flare, the only sign that I've triggered him.

"I need names," he says coolly. "Your father is a lot of things, but he's not a murderer. He didn't act alone. Find out who else was involved."

"Already working on it." I take a breath, then turn away to give myself some space. "My father is a terrible man. He's selfish and rude and belligerent, but until today, I never thought he was evil. I can't have him around my little sister, but she loves her horses too much to leave. Isn't that the dumbest, sweetest thing?" My voice cracks, but I force myself to keep my chin up. "Anyway, Charlie's gonna stay at the house with Livvie until we can figure out what to do about the horses. In the meantime, whatever you do to my dad, just...leave my sisters out of it. Please."

I turn around and Dante is right there, in my space. He cups my chin with his hand and forces me to look up at him. His jaw works to one side, but he says nothing.

Releasing me, he shoves his hands into his pockets. I'm about to leave when he says, "If you're a sommelier, you should make yourself useful in the tasting room. They could use a hand in there."

"I'll be there at eight a.m. sharp."

"Eleven," he corrects, exasperated. "Christ, even the tourists don't drink before noon."

I shoot him a frown. "I'm up at sunrise every day. What the hell am I supposed to do with my mornings?"

"I can think of a few things." He lets loose one of his rare smiles and runs a hand down my arm, his fingers drifting over the sensitive skin on my wrist, drawing out a shiver from me.

"Oh, come on. That's a joke. I'm not sleeping with you."

He takes my hand and presses my palm against his lower abdomen. All at once, I'm completely sober.

"Maybe not. But you will give me a blow job."

"Ha! Now *that's* a joke."

He lowers my hand, over his belt, down the front of

his pants. His cock is thick and stiff, and I grip him through the fabric on instinct, drawing a groan from him.

"That's right. You're going to suck it, Francesca."

Dante reaches out and runs his fingers through my hair, taking firm hold of the strands, tugging just enough to make my scalp tingle. Our eyes lock as he gently, ever so slowly forces me to my knees, holding my gaze the entire time.

The carpet is blessedly thick, and God, so is his cock. My hand is still fondling it.

"Suck it," he repeats. "Right now. Right here. Show me what that hot little mouth is capable of."

I attempt to scoff at him, but nothing comes out. All I can do is lick my lips.

I know I should say no, leave him standing here wanting and alone, but I just can't seem to do it. My mouth is watering, the ache between my legs almost unbearable.

"*Suck*," he commands for the last time.

The tone of his voice makes something inside me snap, and I claw at his zipper hungrily, whimpering when his cock pops free into my eager hand. I lick my lips again to prepare them to receive the fat tip and then I open wide and take him into my mouth, sucking and swirling my tongue around the sensitive skin. I brace myself at first, afraid I'll discover what Jessica may have—the taste of another woman—but I realize quickly that the taste is of him alone.

The salty flavor of his precum flames me on, more evidence of his arousal. I try to take in more and more of him, but there's only so much I can do from this angle, and he's so thick. I look up at his face. My heart blips at the slightest hint of vulnerability I can see there. His eyes are closed, the usual stress lines around his mouth and eyes gone. It makes me want to pounce.

Sliding my lips off of him, hand wrapped firmly around his cock, I get to my feet and force him backwards, one step at a time, stroking him all the while. When the back of his legs hit the couch, I push him into a seated position and drop to my knees in front of him again.

He looks surprised by my aggression, but I'm back on him in an instant, the angle much better as I slide his pants to the floor and suck him all the way to the back of my throat. Dante spreads his legs wider, giving me more room to work. When I reach down to cup his balls, he throws his head back in ecstasy.

Soft sounds come from his throat as I suck, driving me on. I suck harder. I love making him moan. Having this power over him.

I work his balls, tracing them with one finger, trailing my touch beneath his sack to the ultrasensitive skin just below. He sucks in a breath, almost squirming, but doesn't try to stop me. I gently caress that spot, sucking his head hard as I bob back and forth, until he swells in my mouth, stiffening with an agonized grunt. I've got him right on the edge.

He grabs my head and starts thrusting in my mouth, rough, fast, hard. In seconds he's coming, loudly, sounding like he's in pain as he spills his hot seed down my throat. It takes two gulps for me to swallow it all down.

I sit back on my heels, a little dazed. Both of us are breathing hard. My lips are swollen, my jaw aching from all the sucking.

He hasn't moved, as if I've drained the energy straight out of him, but he's staring down at me fiercely. Then he stands, watching me as he fixes his pants. A stone once more. He doesn't offer to help me up, which is fine, because my legs are weak and shaky. I'm not ready yet.

But then he reaches down and puts a hand on my cheek, his thumb tracing my tender lips. "Eleven a.m.," he says.

And then he's gone.

FRANKIE

THANK GOD FOR CANDI.

I spy her getting out of her car in a little black dress and studded Chelsea boots as I make my way down the paved stone walk to the public tasting room at Bellanti Vineyards.

I'm twenty minutes early even after taking extra care with my appearance this morning, dressing in one of my new suits and styling my hair in a long fishtail braid over one shoulder. I kept my makeup light; my aim was to look professional, but very approachable.

Still, my nerves are up—a bit of a jitter in my gut that won't stop. Maybe a quick chat with an old friend will do the trick in settling me down. I'm not sure exactly what I'm nervous about, honestly. Though in the back of my mind, I *do* know. I want to prove myself to Dante, and earn my keep here at the Bellanti estate.

And beyond that, I don't want my husband to regret

giving me this job. Or decide to take it away. Being a kept woman with no occupation was never my goal. The exact opposite, in fact.

"Candi!" I wave, catching her eye.

Her smile is big and welcoming. "Frankie. How are you? Wow, that's an amazing suit."

"Thank you."

I stop next to her on the walk and look down at my clothes, relieved I made the right choice. It only took two hours of changing my mind every few minutes to decide on this outfit. The suit is lavender-and-white striped linen, and underneath I'm wearing a cotton-silk blouse with pintuck detailing. My three-inch nude Manolo Blahniks are fresh out of the box.

"You here on business?" I ask.

"Always," she says.

"Me too. It's my first day on the job. Can I walk you in?"

"Of course," Candi says. "But only if you catch me up on all the hot gossip."

We chat about the goings-on in Napa as we head to the tasting room, neither of us in a hurry. Candi hasn't been to Bella Notte yet, so I recommend it highly. When she asks about my sisters, I give her the rosy version of what they've been up to. The sun is brilliant and pleasantly warm, so we pause outside the tasting room doors for a bit, soaking it up.

The whole time, I debate whether I should tell her about Armani's crush, but I'm not sure I know either of them well enough to play matchmaker just yet. And even though Armani is my favorite Bellanti, he's still a Bellanti —and I know firsthand what being tied to them is like.

"So, how's married life?" she asks.

"What?" Her question pulls me away from the noise in my head. "Oh, it's...well, it's an adjustment."

"Ha! I can imagine. They all seem so aloof and unreadable. Although Armani smiles every now and then. I guess Marco does too, at least when he has a woman on his arm."

"Yeah. And when does he not?" I quip. We laugh. "The little Bellanti definitely has a way with the ladies. But you're right about the unreadable thing. I'm still figuring out Dante."

She's off to check on a delivery, so we say goodbye after making loose plans to get coffee soon. Smoothing my hands down the front of my suit, I take a breath and stride into the tasting room. It's empty save for a middle-aged man with blonde hair and a neatly trimmed beard standing behind the bar. He's in the standard black button-down uniform, with a name tag that says Greg. I approach with a smile and extend a hand.

"Greg, I'm Francesca Bellanti. I'll be the sommelier this afternoon."

He makes no attempt to hide his surprise. "Pleasure to meet you, Mrs. Bellanti. I'm the tasting room manager."

I ignore the stilted way the words tumble from his mouth. I'm getting a bit of a combative vibe from him and

I need to smooth it over. No tension in the tasting room to sour the guests' experiences.

"Thank you, you as well. May I see today's schedule, please?"

He takes a clipboard from the wall behind him. Beautiful wine cases are stacked floor to ceiling behind the bar, and along the far wall of the room, each rack is filled with Bellanti wines. My chest swells at the sight. This is what success looks like. This is what a winery should be: a showcase of hard work, expertise, and delectable craftsmanship.

I thank Greg and take the clipboard. He puts his hands on the bar and watches me as I flip through the pages of wine selections, with fruit and cheese pairings listed beside each one. I pull a pen from my pocket and mull over the wines on the list.

"May I?" I gesture to the wine racks behind the bar.

"Of course. Make yourself at home. I've got a bit to do in the back." His smile is tight as he leaves me.

Taking my time, I look for the bottles on the list, which I pull and set on the bar. Curious about the entire selection available here, I peruse the other vintages around the room and pull a few additional bottles that catch my eye. Before long, I have an impressive row lined up. Considering the fruit and cheeses that are being offered today, I rearrange the line up with the wine I think will pair best and mark my suggested changes on the schedule.

When I'm done, there are only two wines left from the original list. Oops.

But Dante did give me the job, at least for today, so I'm going for it full throttle.

I stand back and look at my selections, nodding approvingly, and then put all the others back. Greg comes in and does a double take at the lineup. He presses his lips into a thin line, as if he's holding himself back from saying what's really on his mind, and then clears his throat.

"None of these are on the schedule, Mrs. Bellanti."

"That is correct. Well, these two are." I tap the corks with my finger.

"Mrs. Bellanti, I've been the tasting room manager for five years. My team and I carefully plan out the daily selections weeks in advance."

I get it. I'm stepping on toes. Too bad, so sad.

"And you and your team obviously do a spectacular job, considering the ongoing success of Bellanti tasting events," I say. "But I couldn't help noticing the framed newspaper article on the wall in the entry that alludes to today's date marking the anniversary of Bellanti Vineyards opening all those years ago. Today is the winery's birthday, if you will."

Greg's brow lifts as if he's not quite following me. "True; however, we only celebrate milestone birthdays. That article marked the 50th. This year is nothing special."

I put up a finger. "I have to disagree. Every year should be celebrated. It's an opportunity to market the history of the wines, and considering that we're coming into fall wedding season, it's the perfect way to cross-market to that demographic. Let our anniversary help celebrate yours...you see what I'm getting at? In fact, there should be a specific selection marketed just for anniversaries."

Frowning, Greg steps in front of me. "Most of what you've chosen is exponentially more expensive than what was on the list. We don't want the guests sampling wines they won't buy."

"Understood. However, the vintages I've chosen—and in this order—tell a much better story of the vineyard, don't you think? From simple table wine to world-renowned blends. If they love it, they'll buy it. Regardless of price."

He crosses his arms, and I know he's not going to see my vision. I'm plowing ahead with it anyway. "But the cost, Mrs. Bellanti. We'll be pouring out hundreds of dollars. Thousands."

"Which means every person who comes through these doors will walk back out with stars in their eyes, knowing firsthand how spectacular our wines are."

Greg is unmoved.

With a sigh, I say, "Fine. Go ahead and dock my pay and I'll cover the cost myself. These *are* our selections."

He doesn't say another word to me as we set up the room.

At 11:30 sharp, he opens the doors to a line of people waiting to get in. It doesn't take long for the room to fill up, guests seated both inside and out on the shaded patio. I work my way from table to table with the waitstaff, describing the wines, tossing out tidbits about the vineyard, and mentioning the winery's anniversary. Outside, a silver-haired couple stops me to ask about the red they're sipping. It's the priciest wine on today's list, but that doesn't stop them from picking my brain about every last nuance and enjoying their glasses to the last drop.

As I stride back inside and join Greg at the bar, I feel a pang of pride. He has a line of guests to ring up for purchases, and to my delight, most every bottle he sells is from the high-end line that I selected. He gives me a side-eye, smiling a little bit, and I take that as a truce.

Just then, the couple I'd been speaking to earlier comes up and orders a few cases of the Elite Reserve— our most expensive wine. For their daughter's upcoming wedding, they tell me, and an extra bottle for their own anniversary at the end of the month.

"How wonderful. Congratulations to your whole family," I say warmly.

Cocking my head, I watch Greg flick his eyes up good-naturedly as he completes the sale and arranges for some of the waitstaff to help load the cases into the couple's car.

"Okay, okay," he finally says. "You were clearly right about the selection and the anniversary thing. I've never had so many people mention the winery's anniversary before."

"Probably because you don't celebrate it. Hopefully, that changes after today."

He laughs. "I'm sure it will." He swipes the credit card of another guest ordering multiple cases of wine, then lowers his voice. "Just between us, we used to have a staff member who did a bang-up job planning the wine lists, but her replacement is a bit of an idiot."

As if on cue, Jessica walks in wearing a dress much too short to do actual work in.

"Speak of the devil," Greg murmurs under his breath.

She makes her way toward us, her expression morphing from cocky confidence to shock as she takes in the open bottles of pricy wine on the bar. Beelining straight to Greg, she scowls as she hisses, "Who's the stupid asshole who fucked up the wine tasting?"

The waitstaff must see the Look in her eye, because they all disappear like roaches when a light goes on. Luckily, the last guest has already wandered to the outside patio—which is a relief, since Jessica wasn't a bit concerned about keeping her voice down.

I cross my hands on the countertop and smile sweetly. "Asshole? Maybe. But stupid, I am not. Is there a problem?"

Jessica's brows shoot up. Apparently, she hadn't noticed me. But she does now.

"Frankie. So good to see you again. And with all your clothes on, for once," she says.

"Well," I say, smile still pasted to my face, "you *do* have to get a little naked for truly mind-blowing sex."

Oh, does that feel good as it comes out of my mouth. Jessica's nostrils flare.

"Not if he's banging you over a desk," she points out.

I nod, pretending to mull it over. So we're doing this. I'm flying pretty high after the successful event, so fine. I'm all in. Leaning over my arms, I say, "That's a great suggestion, sweetie. We don't have a desk in our bedroom, but maybe we'll have to get one."

Greg is looking between us, clearly enjoying the show. He suddenly stiffens and Jessica's entire demeanor changes as Dante strides into the room.

Taking in the scene, he looks at me with one eyebrow hitched. "How's your first tasting going?" he asks.

Jessica tries to put a possessive hand on his arm but he moves away, taking a closer look at the more expensive bottles lined up on the bar just like she did a moment ago.

"Have a look at today's sales receipts," I tell him. I nudge Greg, who prints out a receipt with the grand total and hands it to Dante. He looks over it, then shifts his gaze up to me.

"How did you do this?" he asks.

I shrug. "We uncorked some of the rarer vintages for the lineup, which people seemed to appreciate, and we played up the fact that it's the winery's anniversary today. I suggested we push the Elite Reserve as the perfect anniversary wine. As you can see, the guests agreed."

Dante lowers the paper and smiles.

It's a real smile, a rare one, both ends of his lips curving up. My heart flips and I can't help but smile back, even though his quickly disappears again.

He leans over the bar and gives me a kiss on the cheek. His lips linger, his voice low so only I can hear. "Don't forget, you have work to do on that *other* project as well."

Then he kisses me again, his warm lips pressed

against my temple. I pull in a breath as sweet warmth cascades over me. He winks as he walks away.

When I turn back to Jessica, I realize this entire day was worth it.

She's positively green with envy.

It is perfection.

FRANKIE

"We have a problem."

Charlie's voice trembles slightly when she says it. She's still at Dad's house with Livvie. I called right after my latest shift in the tasting room to check in, and now I'm sitting in the swivel chair by the window in my bedroom, a pair of sweatpants waiting for me on the bed.

"Do I want to know?" I ask. I get the feeling I'm about to hear something a lot more serious than whatever gossip kept them up all night. Whenever my sister loses the lightness in her voice, I know something is up.

"Dad didn't come home last night. I've been calling and texting him for hours with no response. Have you heard from him?"

"No. But that's not unusual, Char."

She's right to be worried, though. Our dad is shady as fuck, but he's a homebody. No matter what kind of trouble he gets up to, he always comes home, parks himself in front of the TV, and does the tango with a twelve-pack and a liter. Growing up, I can barely remember a time when he wasn't passed out on the couch by ten p.m.

"It's weird," Charlie goes on. "I heard him leave late yesterday like he was in a hurry, kicking up gravel and revving the engine. He never said anything about where he was going."

My chest squeezes. "Did you check his office? Anything missing?"

"Not that I could tell. His desk calendar is there with nothing written on it. Desk is locked up, though I wouldn't know what to look for anyway. You know how Dad is."

"Yeah." Secretive. Conniving. Often paranoid.

As it turns out, probably for good reasons.

Letting out a breath, I put the phone on speaker and tap out a text to Donovan, asking him if he can drive me around for a few hours. "What does Livvie think?"

"I haven't told her anything yet. I don't want her to worry."

"Good. Listen, I'm gonna cruise around. Hit up his usual spots. Racetracks, bars, maybe some nightclubs. See if I can find him, ask around in case anyone's heard anything."

There's a pause and then Charlie's voice drops low, measured, as if she doesn't want to be overhead. "Do you think it's a good idea for you to go poking around alone?"

Fair point. A lot of the places our dad likes to hang out wouldn't be safe for an MMA fighter, much less a woman alone. "I won't be alone," I tell her. "I'll have Donovan with me."

"You mean...Dante's spy who acts as your chauffeur?"

"Yeah. That's the one. He's really very sweet, though," I insist.

Charlie pauses again and I can virtually hear the wheels turning in her mind. "Fine, but make sure you turn your location on in HeyYou so I can see where you are, just in case."

Sometimes the three of us use this app called HeyYou to send silly pictures and short videos back and forth, though Charlie and I are too busy to use it much and Livvie runs circles around us with it. It has a setting that allows you to choose which friends can see your location. I usually keep it on for my sisters, and they do the same for me. Like Charlie said, just in case.

I check the app. "It's on. Talk to you soon. Call me if you hear from him. Love you."

"Love you."

After we hang up, I call Donovan and ask him to bring the car around to the front door. It's almost two, and I'm still dressed for work in a crisp suit—which doesn't seem like the best choice for poking around my dad's stomping grounds. I quickly change into black skinny jeans, a plain tee shirt, and sneakers, and twist my hair into a braid. Then I grab a notepad and pen and rush downstairs and out the door.

When I slide into the car, I don't miss the curious look Donovan gives me.

"Change of plans today. I need you to take me to the racetrack. And some other places."

He grins. "I'd love nothing more, Mrs. Bellanti."

Anxiety grips me, and while I appreciate the light teasing in his words, I just want to get going. "Great, then let's go." I wait until he's situated in the front seat, then lean forward and check out the list I'm furiously scribbling. "Breezeway racetrack first, then Sonoma."

He puts the car into drive. "Feeling lucky today?"

Don't I wish.

The track is only marginally occupied, most people at the bar having a drink and something to eat. The race schedule is light considering it's a weekday. Not my father's normal time to be here. He prefers the bigger races, the rowdier crowds, so he has an excuse to drink more. Knowing it's likely futile, I scour the restaurant, the bar, and the stands. The barns are nearly empty, as is every other place he might be in the damned complex.

Before I leave, I give my dad's cell a call. I hear one ring before I get sent to voicemail. My hairline tingles. Either his phone has been shut off or it's dead.

Frustrated, though not surprised, I leave and have Donovan take me to my father's second favorite racetrack in Sonoma. There's not a lot going on, save for the usual suspects bellied up to the bar. After checking all the places I can think of, I return to the car and we hit the strip of bars and nightclubs my father likes to frequent. But most of his favorite haunts aren't open this early in the day. The ones that are offer a handful of people who claim to know nothing. I skip out of each establishment as quick as I can, not wanting to push my luck on this side of town.

Back at the Abbott compound, I go directly to my father's shambles of an office. Looking for anything that could tell me who the car tamperer was, or where my dad might be, I begin a divide and conquer of every drawer and cabinet I can get into. Some of the desk drawers are locked and I'm tempted to break into them, but I think about the repercussions if, when, my dad suddenly shows up again. Knowing him, he's probably just sleeping it off on some random woman's couch and he'll stumble in when he's sober enough.

I tell myself this, but my heart doesn't believe it.

"Hey." Charlie's voice startles me. She's standing in the doorway, holding a tray of tea and cookies. "I've already been through all of this. Did you find anything?"

The bite of frustrated tears irritates my eyes. "Nada. Not a damn thing. No one has seen him, he's not at the track, and there's nothing here but an empty calendar, a bunch of overdue bills, and a pile of empty beer cans under his desk."

Our eyes meet and the depth of my concern is mirrored back at me by my sister. She tilts her head. "Come on. Let's have a drink on the balcony. Best view in the whole joint."

And it is. I cross the room and open the doors to the balcony, and we step out into the sun. It's warm and everything is golden and bright. Livvie is riding in the paddock, blonde ponytail bouncing in time with the horse's hoofbeats.

Charlie sets the tray on a metal bistro table and pours the tea for us. Hugging myself, I soak up the sun while taking in what a dilapidated, sad mess the winery's grounds are. The paddock where Livvie rides is surrounded by a fence that's sagging and crooked. The back of the barns are visible from here, the wood terribly aged, peeling and broken in many places. Nothing is tended. Everything is overgrown. It's the perfect picture of neglect, and it hurts to see it.

Charlie hands me a steaming cup. "A couple contacted me the other day about having their wedding here."

I arch a brow. "Really?"

She makes a face. "Yup. They'd heard about the *fabulous* grounds and thought it would be wonderful to get married at a historic winery like this one."

"Oh dear. So what happened?"

She takes a small sip. "They took one look at the place in person and very quickly backed out. I don't think they were even here for ten minutes. Not that I blame them."

We both sigh. This scenario is easy to imagine. I mean, just look at this place. It's literally falling apart. The buildings are historic, but they're about to be old piles of wood and brick if something doesn't turn around.

"I'm sorry," I say. "I know what it would mean for your wedding planning business if you could use this place as a venue."

"Yeah. It'd be great to actually get to do some work. Oh well."

178

She shrugs and sips her tea while leaning over the balcony railing. I move next to her and we look down below at Livvie on her huge black horse. He's moving around the ring with a high step trot while our little sister sits tall in the saddle, her back straight, arms up and out as she holds the reins.

I can almost read the guilt that I know is playing through Charlie's head right now. She'd love this place to be fabulous for our little sister. The barns returned to their glory, the grounds perfectly manicured and tended. Hell, I'd settle with functional. A barn that Livvie wouldn't have to try to fix herself in order to keep her horses comfortable. A house with appliances that work and floors that don't bow and flex when you walk across them.

Smiling at Livvie, Charlie says, "I guess the Abbott sisters just get better with every version that comes out, right? Maybe if you and I work hard enough, she'll get to have a happy ending of her own someday."

"That's not fair to you, Char. You had to be a mom for all of us when ours walked out. You never had time for yourself or your own dreams. Mom and Dad failed us. You didn't."

I finish my drink, wishing there were something stronger in it than raspberry tea. Charlie's got that far-off look on her face. It's her standard expression when she's mentally beating herself up.

I lean my head on her shoulder. She smells like subtle citrusy perfume and fresh laundry. "Hey," I say. "In my eyes, you were the best big sister anyone could ask for."

She smiles and the teacup shakes slightly in her hand. There's a beat of silence as we watch Livvie slow the horse to a walk.

"We're going to try for a baby."

Pulling back from her shoulder, I look at my sister to see if she's pranking me. Her smile grows and when she looks at me, I notice the smile reaches her eyes. "Wow."

"Yeah, we decided it's time. I mean, I'm a little apprehensive about it—I know it's not ideal, having a child when your family's in the mob, but...I know he'll be a great dad."

She sets down her cup on the table. I'm not sure how to respond. I want to be happy for her. I *am* happy for her. If this is what she wants, then yes! But it's hard for me to know sometimes if Charlie is doing things for herself or for others. She's lived a huge part of her life for other people—Livvie and me, our dad. Her husband.

"Have you and Dante talked about having kids?" she asks.

"He mentioned heirs once, but we haven't really talked about anything seriously. Seems we don't have that kind of relationship. I think I would like kids someday, though."

The horse comes to a choppy halt in the center of the ring. Livvie pats his neck, leaning forward to coo something in his ear.

"It's just...when I pictured my life, I always imagined babies. But I never imagined a husband like Dante. I imagined...love."

Charlie stares at me intently. It's not like she got the

husband of her dreams, either. She and I are on a parallel path when it comes to the arranged marriage bullshit.

She doesn't say anything. Maybe I touched a nerve.

We both turn back to watching Livvie as she cues the horse into a rocking canter. She pulls the reins ever so slightly, asking the horse to change his gait into a delayed, long-legged stride. "She's something special, isn't she?" I say softly.

"She is." Charlie grips the balcony rail with one hand until her knuckles turn white. "What if Dad comes back with a husband for Livvie?"

My hairline tingles, a lump forming in my throat at the thought. "Nothing like that is ever going to happen to her. *Ever*."

"Okay." Charlie nods in agreement. "Not ever."

I put my hand over hers to seal our vow. "Not ever."

20

FRANKIE

FOR THE FIRST time in weeks, I'm completely alone, with no agenda and no eyes on me. It might only be for a little while, but as I run through the vineyard in the blue-gray of predawn, the cool morning air filling my lungs, I'm grateful for the time to do something for myself. I'd almost forgotten what it was like.

Running makes me feel free in a way that nothing else does. I love the powerful ability of my legs to move me across the ground, my feet hitting the packed earth between the vines while kicking up the scents of a fresh new day. It reminds me of Italy. I'd wake with the sun and stretch on the cobblestone path outside my building, then run the well-worn trail through an olive grove that led to a hay field, a dirt road, and finally ended at the *pasticceria* just outside of the village. Who doesn't love ending their run at the doorstep of a pastry shop?

Sadly, my run today won't end with a cornetto and a latte in my hand. I don't have the pleasure of those sweet things in my life at the moment. I have a philandering husband, instead. A controlling, philandering husband who is only begrudgingly starting to see me as a person (wow, what a hero), and a missing, possibly endangered father who traded his daughter for a few creature comforts—and is likely making a similar arrangement for his youngest daughter, too.

Thank God I have my sisters.

At the top of a rise, I stop to take pleasure in watching the sun peek over the horizon, spilling soft light onto the vines. My breaths come hard, punctuating the dark thoughts in my mind. So much for endorphins making me feel good. Reality is stronger than hormones, I guess.

Focusing on my breathing, I take off again through the rows.

I reflect more on my two beautiful sisters who are trying so hard to make the best out of the shitty family life we grew up with. Not only was our mother gone and our father emotionally checked out or drunk all the time, but school was always rough for Charlie and me, too. Not because we struggled academically but because making friends was impossible.

For some reason, us older Abbott girls had a reputation for being stuck up bitches, even though any "attitude" we had was just shyness and a lingering embarrassment about our home life. It didn't help that Charlie was such a knockout with her long legs and golden hair, or that I was in a C-cup bra by the time I was twelve; we both had to deal with boys making relentless passes at us (whether we reciprocated or not, the term *slut* seemed to follow us like a shadow).

With Livvie, though, it's different. She's so warm and friendly and bubbly that she has more friends than she can keep track of. She's easy to love. Nobody shuns her or graffitis her locker or writes her number in the boys' bathroom stalls. And I couldn't be more happy for her. I'm glad she'll never feel isolated the way I did, the way Charlie did. Things aren't all bad.

I have my job, too, I suppose. It's a job I would normally love, but it being tied up with so many strings and limitations...it just feels like one more link in the chains holding me down.

My legs muscles relax as I finally find a rhythm. My pulse beats steadily against my neck. My breathing is paced. There's a stand of cypress trees to the right, far beyond the vines, but similar enough to the landscape of Tuscany that nostalgia washes over me.

The heady, almost sweet scent of the trees. The crunch of detritus on the path under my feet. My chest swells again, with longing this time. I've only been away from Italy a short while, but it feels so much longer. My life there was busy, but...uncomplicated.

A pair of brown eyes flash in my mind's eye. Rico was definitely not uncomplicated.

Steeling my jaw, I will the image away. Rico is out of my life now, for a reason, and it's going to stay that way.

Suddenly, my motivation to run is stripped away. Dammit. Rico was a mistake. I made a few mistakes in

Italy—and I can admit I've made a few since coming back, too—but I don't have to keep making them.

I'm tired of men running my life. My father, Rico, Dante. I've been at a man's whim in one shape or form my entire life. I'm fucking done.

Slowing to a jog, I try to recenter my thoughts and concentrate on the exercise, but the moment is lost. And I can't stop stressing about the fact that Dad is still missing in action. I head into the house and shower, letting the hot water sluice over me and loosen my muscles.

I get out, dry off, and get ready for work, but the winery won't be open to guests for a few hours and I'm all wound up now. I figure I might as well take advantage of the early morning quiet and see about maximizing the visual aesthetic of the tasting room.

When I get there, I revel in the quietness of the empty room for a moment before flicking on the lights, setting my purse behind the bar, and making a fresh pot of coffee. Sipping with my elbows on the counter, I survey the space. Something about this room bothered me the very first time I'd walked in here, but I hadn't taken the time to figure out what it was. Now, it hits me almost immediately as I drink my coffee.

The flow is all wrong. Customers come in through the French doors to find huge display stands on either side of them, blocking their view of the rest of the room. Once past the displays, they have to maneuver around a small table with a massive floral arrangement, which is elegant, but also blocks the view. It's not until they get around all of these obstacles that the presentation of

185

wines along the bespoke shelving on the brick walls come into view.

Unfortunately, the harsh overhead track lighting is angled directly on the bottles. Which, I get it. The better to illuminate what we're trying to sell. But it's not at all subtle. In fact, it gives the room a cold, commercial vibe. Like this is a liquor store, and the only thing we're interested in is maximizing wine sales.

This is a *tasting room*. People should walk in and immediately feel relaxed, embraced by sophisticated but comfortable design, as if we're welcoming them into our home for a repast. Because we are. We're not just selling them wine, we're selling them an experience. A story.

In fact, looking closer at the walls, I can see the brick itself telling a story. I reach out and run my palm over a large stained section. It's mostly hidden behind a bistro table topped by an urn of pampas grass and spiky dried thistles. I grimace. That ugly arrangement has Jessica written all over it. Whoever put this here has done the winery a huge disservice—that stained brick is an important part of the Bellanti story.

I'd done my research when I found out I was marrying into the family, of course. A fire nearly a century ago had nearly ruined the winery before it could really get started. The fire had started in a storage room, damaging several barrels of aging wine. Luckily, after consuming most of the available oxygen in the space, it had died down, enabling workers to extinguish it. An entire wall of brick had been scarred, but some of it had been salvaged and repurposed when this area of the house was constructed.

Setting down my coffee, I wrangle the urn away from the wall and lug it behind the counter, then clear the bistro table and move it out of the way, too.

There are several bottles of Pinot Noir in the basement vault which had been aging at the time of the fire. A handful of the original barrels are still in use today, producing delicious Pinot which we could offer on display along with a catchy story about the fire. I put the table back for the time being, but the wheels are turning on how to revamp this entire section.

Continuing my perusal, I walk the room, noting several seating options are in the way of the flow of the room. Three chaise lounges near the picture window impede flow to the wine cases on either side. Free standing racks of upsell merchandise aren't very visible to guests unless they are specifically looking. Nope, nope, and nope.

Before I realize it, the morning has passed. I have a list of notes by the time employees start to filter into the room. Greg is looking at his phone as he automatically heads to the bar.

"Morning, Greg."

His head snaps up, cheeks going pink as he hurriedly puts his phone in his pocket.

"Mrs. Bellanti. I didn't see you there." His forehead wrinkles as he looks at the slight mess I've made in the room rearranging the displays. "What's...going on?"

I point to the clipboard and the list I started.

"Improvements. I'd like to change a few more things around before we open today. To promote better circulation of the visitors and draw the eye to the wines without relying on these harsh track lights."

"I see." He picks up the clipboard, lips pursed. "Well. We'd best get started, then."

Greg trusts me. I'm grinning from ear to ear. "Let's."

Just then, two young women walk in wearing white button-downs with the Bellanti logo, black pants, and black aprons. They notice my mess immediately and turn to Greg.

"Good morning, ladies. We're going to help Mrs. Bellanti move a few things around before we open the doors this morning."

An older man walks in wearing the same uniform. He frowns as he ties on his apron, as if it's a necessary evil that he really doesn't enjoy. I'm not sure why our showroom staff need to look like everyday waiters. Sure, they serve cheese and fruit plates with the wine, but they aren't standard food service workers; they're experts on Bellanti wine. Specially trained connoisseurs. I make yet another mental note to see how Dante feels about changing the uniform.

"Good morning, everyone." I make quick introductions. "We have roughly one hour before opening. Here's what I'd like to do, quickly, so there's still time for pre-opening tasks."

Soon, the entire tasting room staff is involved. Once the larger pieces are in place, I can refine the smaller things later, like the upsell merchandise. Everyone gets to work rearranging. Greg stops me and hesitantly suggests swapping out the large chairs in front of the fireplace for smaller ones so more guests can see and enjoy the stone hearth and aged mahogany mantle.

"Love it. Let's do it."

He eyes me. "Really?"

"It's exactly what I'm aiming for. An upscale experience on every level."

Greg nods. "I can't tell you how often I see visitors just standing around the fireplace, trying to enjoy the ambience but with nowhere to sit. Those two armchairs are never open."

We make the swap, managing to fit a wood bench, two sleek side chairs, and an upholstered ottoman that doubles as extra seating. And he was right. What a difference.

One of the women, Nia, suggests getting rid of a rack holding wine openers with the Bellanti Vineyards logo and instead placing them in baskets stacked in a tier by the register. The baskets are woven with black metal handles, and the wine openers look eye-catching in them.

"This looks fabulous," I tell her. "I'm so glad you suggested it. Genius."

"Thank you. And thanks for listening," she says shyly. "Not exactly something we're used to from the upper management."

Something tells me she's referring to Jessica, but I don't pry. We fill the remaining baskets with upsell merchandise, realign the chaise loungers, and rearrange the floral bouquets.

With minutes to spare, we stand in a line and admire our work. The change is inspiring. The whole room is visible, the lighting more gentle, the setup inviting guests to wander around, browse the wines, sit and enjoy the fireplace or the view from the window.

"This is so great!" I tell everyone. "Thank you all for your Herculean efforts."

I give them each a high five. Every single employee is genuinely smiling. I know they have more setup to do before the doors open, so I gather up my clipboard and coffee cup.

"Before you go, I have a list of things I'll be speaking to Mr. Bellanti about. Is there anything you all need that would make your jobs easier?"

A stunned sort of silence falls as the employees look at each other. Sensing their uncertainty, I gesture to the aprons.

"I'm going to start with your uniforms. You need something a little less 'service staff.' You're all experts in Bellanti wine, so your presentation should reflect the hard work you've put in to earn that status. I know the training isn't easy."

"That's an understatement," Nia says.

They look at each other, and one of the men speaks up. "Maybe we could get some of those mats that you stand on to keep your legs and feet from dying by the end of the day?"

"Anti-fatigue mats. Definitely a yes. Got it," I say, nodding as I add it to the list.

"What about a few stools for the staff?" someone else

suggests. "We wouldn't sit when it's busy, obviously. But when there aren't visitors, we have to lean on the bar because there's nowhere for us to sit down and rest. I've got arthritis in my back, so it would really help."

"Gosh, of course," I say. "I'm sorry nobody addressed that yet—I promise there will be stools in here within the next day or so. This isn't a torture chamber. What else?"

Greg looks at his workers, but it seems they're out of ideas for now. "We'll let you know if anything else comes to mind. Thank you, Mrs. Bellanti."

We part ways and I turn to the wine list for today's tastings. I feel proud as I pull bottles and work on the arrangement. I'm excited to see how the flow goes when guests begin arriving.

Plus, I think I'm well on my way to earning the staff's undying loyalty.

21

FRANKIE

I CHECK my phone and read a few texts from Charlie, but she says there's been no word about our father. Determined not to lose the high I'm on from a successful morning, I double-check the list I just made as I walk into the main offices, mentally calculating what the promises I'd just made to the staff will cost. It's relatively little compared to the energy and allegiance we'll get in return from happy employees, but I know I'll still have to justify the purchases to Dante.

"Afternoon, Mrs. Bellanti."

"Hi, Ruby. How are you?"

Ruby is keeping watch from her perch behind the reception desk. Unlike the first time I was here, she smiles at me and gives a little wave. I like to think my charming personality made her come around, but I know it's the Chanel scarf I left in a gift bag for her as a peace offering. She's been eating out of my hand ever since.

I smile at her and make my way down the hall to

Dante's office. I'm going to have to sweet talk him a little, be suave. He's not one to think about other people's comfort, and if he does, it doesn't seem to be a high priority for him.

His door is partially open, so I sail right in, not bothering to knock.

The smell of heavy perfume hits me, and I look automatically toward the desk. Dante is leaning way back in the chair, Jessica practically straddling him with one leg wedged between his thighs, her other foot on the floor. Her tongue is down his throat, her hand over his crotch.

The clipboard almost falls from my hand, but I grip it so hard the edge digs into my palm.

Jessica pulls back, her teasing voice just loud enough for me to hear. "Come on, lover. We'd have a beautiful baby together."

Jesus fucking Christ. My limbs feel heavy and numb as I back out of the room and walk numbly into the restroom, locking the door and sliding down the cool tiled wall with the clipboard clutched to my chest. I can't breathe. I'm suffocating, drowning. Anxiety rises up inside me, floods me until I'm shaking.

Pulling breaths through my nose, I throw the clipboard across the room, watching it clatter to the floor. I *knew* he was an asshole. I *knew* he was cheating on me. And with his assistant of all people—God, what a cliché. But none of this is news to me.

So why *the fuck* do I feel this rage? Why do I still let him get to me? I'm sick of it. Sick of letting him dictate everything. Sick of men controlling my entire life.

I can't believe I actually thought I might be able to lift up the edges of his controlling, self-absorbed, egotistical bullshit of a personality. What did all my effort get me anyway, besides a front-row seat to another woman's hand on my husband's cock? Was I seriously entertaining the notion that I could change him? Men don't change— at least, not men like him. He takes what he wants without a hint of guilt or a second thought. With no shame, no regard for anyone else's feelings, and certainly without a worry of getting caught.

It's time to set some boundaries, once and for all. Except that every time I try, my body betrays me. I need to pull myself together. March back in there and exercise some self-control.

Smoothing my hair, taking a deep breath, I close my eyes and will myself to calm down. I've got this. I have a job to do and I'm going to do it. Not my problem if Dante is interrupting his workday to get laid. Now I'm going to interrupt his getting laid with work.

When I get back to his office, clipboard in hand, Jessica is nowhere to be seen. Well, at least I won't have to confront my husband and his mistress at the same time.

Dante looks up from his computer, his annoyed expression deepening when he sees that it's me. He can be as annoyed as he wants. I'm not leaving until I've said my piece.

I shut the door pointedly behind me. The snick of the lock sliding into place unleashes something in me. It takes a second to realize what it is.

The absence of fear.

"You listen to me." I approach his desk and slap the clipboard down. His eyes snap to mine with a warning glare. I could not care less. "I don't give two fucks what you do on company time, even though everyone knows that fucking your assistant is generally considered bad business practices—not to mention a pathetic cliché. *However—*"

I only pause to take a quick breath. Now that I've started, I can't seem to stop.

"You will *not* bring a child into this nightmare, you understand? Jessica is a conniving bitch who'd use any child you two had as a pawn, guaran-fucking-teed. It's exactly how my sisters and I grew up—nothing but pawns between our parents until Mom finally walked out, leaving us to be bargaining chips for our father. But I guess you know all about that, don't you?"

A muscle works in his jaw. I stab my finger in the air at him.

"Maybe you can't keep yourself from sticking your dick in other women, but I am putting my foot down about you having children out of wedlock. So you *better* wear a damn condom when you're fucking around."

Picking up the clipboard, I turn to leave, but he's way too fast and grabs my wrist. I didn't even hear him get out of the chair before his fingers closed hard around the delicate bones. Dante holds my gaze as he walks around the desk to face me. His body is brimming with anger, the heat of it sizzling around him. I'm still not afraid. I'm incensed.

He grins humorlessly. "Aren't you a jealous bitch. You're the only one allowed to have my children, then?"

I let out a low laugh. "I don't want anything from you, certainly not a child. The world needs less Bellanti assholes in it, not more."

Pulling my wrist away, I turn for the door. But he grabs the clipboard and tosses it across the desk, then pulls me into his arms, wrapping them around me. The moment he lifts my chin and looks at my mouth, I know I'm in trouble.

"Oh, you definitely want something from me," he says. "You know exactly what you want from me."

"I don't." I try to say it with conviction, even as my voice cracks and my knees go weak.

"Liar."

His hand slides over my abdomen, as if feeling for his child. Then it slips down the waistband of my skirt, into my panties, dipping into the shameful wetness that's gathered between my legs. When he plunges two fingers inside me all at once, I can't help but moan.

Damn, damn, *damn* my stupid body for betraying me again.

The instant shock of pleasure jolts the fight right out of me. I sink into his touch, hating myself as I do it, but powerless to stop it. He doesn't make a sound as he begins a fast, powerful assault on my clit. In seconds, I'm panting and grinding against his hand. My orgasm builds fast and potent, but he stills his fingers before I can come, as if he knew I was about to and couldn't wait to deny me.

A sound of protest works from my lips. Satisfied with

whatever I just proved to him, he spins me around and shoves me facedown onto the desk, yanking up my skirt. My palms go flat on the surface as he presses into me from behind, trapping me. A deep ache throbs in my pussy as Dante grinds his hard cock against my ass.

I push back against him, telling myself it's to force him away, though it's really because I need to feel his dick inside me.

He doesn't make me wait.

Tugging the crotch of my panties to the side, he plunges into me, filling me. I moan again—I can't help it—and he begins to thrust. I meet him thrust for thrust, wanting more, wanting it deeper, harder. More.

I hate myself for this. For letting him end every argument and solve every fight by fucking me into silence.

Or submission.

His body arches over mine, pinning me, making me helpless to do anything except receive his thick cock. I reach behind me and tangle my fingers in his hair, twisting my head to kiss him, holding him as tightly as he's holding me. In a rush, my orgasm is back on the verge. He jackhammers into me, using me like I'm his personal fuck doll, pounding faster and faster, the edge of the desktop cutting into the tops of my thighs. His hand comes down to smack my ass with a sharp slap.

The bite of pain throws me over. I come hard, almost screaming out my pleasure, but I catch myself and whimper as the ecstasy floods me.

Dante wraps a hand around my throat, thrusts hard twice, and spills his seed into me. It shoots hard and hot, deep inside, and in that moment, I know that it's over. This rush of madness that takes away all the anger and hatred I feel for him has passed—and the moment I right my skirt and sweep back my hair, we'll be right where we left off.

Dante pulls out and steps back, but I don't get up. I lie there, half on his desk, my bare ass in the air. I don't want to face him. Face the fact that, once again, I allowed him to manipulate me into silence.

I hate him.

I hate myself.

Worse? I hate that Jessica was right about the mind-blowing sex on a desk.

Being sure not to look at Dante, I finally stand and situate my clothes, feeling him start to drip out of me. I look over at him, shaking my head. His hands are in his trouser pockets, his face expressionless.

My voice fills with acid. "Why are you like this? How can this possibly make you happy?"

For a half-second, I swear I catch a beat of discomfort flash across his face. A flicker of vulnerability. Maybe even...shame. But his mask comes down again, and with his clothes back in place, he stalks out of the office without another word.

22

DANTE

Fucking hell, women are a nuisance.

I'd hired Jessica two years ago because she was good at keeping track of my calendar, and *really* good at sucking me off under my desk. But she seems to keep forgetting that our relationship is a business arrangement —not a personal one. For the first time since I brought her on, I'm seriously starting to regret hiring her at all.

True, I've used Jessica to my advantage. More than once, I've flirted with another woman just to get her to agree to something filthy I wanted to do in bed. It's been surprisingly easy. It's *always* been easy to bend Jessica to my whims, and never once have I worried about her feelings. As for her, I know she hopes to get more from me than a signature on her paychecks. She made it clear on day one that she'd happily do whatever it took to move up the company ranks.

But ever since my new wife entered the picture, Jessica has become insanely possessive. She isn't just pandering to me like usual. She's holding nothing back in her bid for my attention, her jealousy over my wife unbecoming in a causal sex partner and flat out unacceptable in an employee. It's made me realize that her cheap tricks are exactly that.

It doesn't seem to matter that I haven't slept with my assistant since I got married—it only seems to spur Jessica on even more in her efforts to get me back into bed. I'm not even sure if this is about me at all, or if Jessica's just trying to prove something. To *win*.

Which is a losing game, because I'm the one with all the power around here. And I wouldn't touch that pussy again with a ten-foot pole.

Not because of my wife, obviously. I can still do whatever I want with whomever I want; the marriage is a sham anyway. But sex with Francesca is...it's different.

Because I can do whatever I want with her. *To* her. She's nothing like Jessica. Nothing like any woman I've ever fucked before. And the way she takes her own pleasure...it somehow makes mine even more fulfilling.

Fuck, that's stupid. Sex is just sex. Love is for people without a plan.

Walking the stone path to the tasting room, I check my phone for messages and reply to a few but my mind isn't fully focused on what I'm typing. I can't stop thinking about Francesca bent over my desk, her legs spread wide, her skin flushed, her eyes flashing those damn daggers at me. God, the way she looks at me. The way she fights me, tooth and nail, in our lives *and* in bed

—every time I take her, in fact. She hates me. Yet she never says no. It's so fucking hot, I—

No, I'm not going there. Who cares why it's different with Francesca? I'm overthinking it, something I never used to do until I married her.

Opening the tasting room doors, I step into the show-room and stop dead in my tracks, momentarily confused. It looks like I've walked into the wrong building.

Ridiculous. Of course I haven't. But the room is completely rearranged. Who the hell did this? Nobody came to me to ask for permission. And I sure as hell didn't approve it.

The room is free of guests at the moment but there's another tasting soon. I see employees milling around, tidying, adding bottles to shelves while talking to each other. They're working, sure, but I notice they seem more relaxed than usual. They're...are they...smiling?

They are. And not in that polite, polished, retail worker way that I demand from all my public-facing employees. These are real, actual smiles.

"Hello, Mr. Bellanti," someone says quietly, but I wave them away dismissively.

Clasping my hands behind my back, I start a slow walk around the room, taking in the changes. I realize instantly that the place just...looks better. Somehow. The flow is better, the arrangement of the furniture and acces-sories are more inviting. The staff turn and watch me, their happy expressions fading, their conversations dying off. It's like they disappear when I appear, turning brittle and giving me the plastic versions of themselves. Flashing the same stilted smiles that everyone gives me—a little nervous, a little too big. And completely fake.

Greg, the manager, gives me a hesitant wave of greeting. He's been here for years, and it bothers me that he's still uncomfortable around me. Perhaps I haven't given the best impression to my staff. Not that I've paid much attention. That's been Jessica's department for a while now.

I give Greg a nod in return and do my best to appear unintimidating, though I'm not sure how I'm supposed to pull that off. I move my hands from behind my back and take a more causal pose as I finish my walkthrough.

The changes are impressive, and I decide that I approve. Though I can't say for sure, I suspect my wife is behind this development. If so, she's caught my attention twice now when it comes to the family business. Maybe I've been too reluctant to give her some rein, though I'll have to wait and see what else she has up her sleeve before deciding.

I realize just then that the staff have paused in their work to look at me, as if waiting for some kind of reaction from me. So I check my watch, then give them all a nod. "The room opens again in ten minutes, and everything had better be in place when it does. Back to work. Now."

Striding out, I start to head back in the direction of my office, but quickly change my mind. Francesca likely still there, and I don't want to deal with any more of her accusations right now. I sent Jessica to the house earlier to pick up a file I'd left in my room, and I really don't want to run into her, either. Being caught between these women is making me feel...less in control. And I may not be a lot of things, but I'm *always* in control.

Guess it's time for a surprise inspection at the vats, then.

Slipping into my car, I drive to the heart of the winery. The familiar long, low, steel building makes me feel instantly calmer. This is where Bellanti wines are made, and immersing myself in the process has always brought me peace. I'll do a walkthrough of the press before I inspect the vats, maybe take a sample or two of the wines coming out of aging. I haven't had a chance to taste the product from last year's harvest, and it's a family tradition to drink some before the vats are prepared for the current season. This preparation includes making sure the vats are scrubbed to an exacting standard before the harvest begins in earnest next month.

But my brother Marco is in charge of it—and God knows he always needs a supervisor. Which is exactly why I need to check up on things. With all the time he spends chasing tail, I wouldn't be surprised if he hasn't set foot in this building in weeks. At least not for anything other than copious amounts of "taste testing."

I park my car outside the steel structure but I don't move to get out. Instead, I find myself yet again thinking about my wife. She hasn't toured this building yet, as far as I know. I should bring her here, give her the full tour, considering she's hell-bent on being a part of the business.

A groan works from my throat as I flash back to the blow job she gave me the other night. Unbidden, the images play out in my mind like a porno. Her eyes looking up at me as she sucked me off. The way she pushed me onto the couch and dropped to her knees. Fuck, she's got a hot little mouth. My cock twitches at the phantom feel of her tongue circling my head, sucking hard on my shaft. There's an innocence in the way she touches me, in the sounds she makes while I'm fucking her. Like sex is something new to her.

It's not that she's actually inexperienced—more that she isn't experienced in the way she wants me to believe. She might be a little hellcat, but when it comes to sex, Francesca is learning the depths of her lust for the first time. Virgin or not, this passion is new to her. It's obvious to me that I'm the first to draw it out. That nobody has ever fucked her like I do.

I swallow hard and twist my thoughts away. If I keep this up, I'm going to have to find my wife and throw her over my desk again.

The winery is running like clockwork as I wander through. Staff pause to greet me, but otherwise don't turn from their work. Which is exactly as it should be. They've got more important things to do than kiss my ass.

When I finally sit in the dim light of the cellar to mull over a glass of wine from last year's harvest, my mind instantly wanders back to Francesca.

I already gave her the AmEx and the Jag back. She has unlimited funds, a name that has clout both in Napa and around the world. A massive house full of domestic workers (and a personal chef) ready to jump at her every whim. She has everything, including my blessing to work here at Bellanti Vineyards. She certainly doesn't need to use sex to get what she wants from me. It's all been handed to her already. So why is she acting the way she is?

The woman is a puzzle.

I lean back in my chair and stare blankly at the cellar wall. Could it be that my wife just...likes having sex with me? That she doesn't want anything in return?

Does she actually want...to be with me?

It's a good thing I'm alone in the cellar, because I laugh out loud. What a ridiculous thought. When has a woman ever had a legitimate interest in me, and not what I could give her?

Tossing back the rest of my wine, I head to the vats for my inspection. I take the maintenance sheets from their hook on the wall and go through them page by page. Then I visit each vat, making sure they've been prepped and prepared to receive the influx of product coming their way. Before I realize it, an hour has passed, and I haven't thought about my personal life for one second of that time. Escape from one's burdens—this is the boon of being a workaholic.

The moment I'm finished, though, the familiar restlessness comes back.

I want to blame it on Jessica, on my shitshow of a marriage, on Marco's even-more-selfish-than-usual behavior lately, on the lingering shadow of my father's death and the fact that I'll likely be avenging his murder if my wife can dig up some names...but none of those things are what's really bothering me.

I look to the ceiling and take a breath.

For the first time in a very long time, and for some unknowable reason, I've somehow let emotions get past my walls. There's a crack in my armor. And now I feel the weight of something I haven't allowed myself to acknowledge since I was a child.

I miss my mother.

23

FRANKIE

THE DAYS PASS, and there's still no sign of my dad. The more time that goes by, the more sinister his disappearance seems. The harder it gets to tell myself there wasn't any foul play.

It's not just that he's missing, either. There is literally no sign of him anywhere, or any clue to tip us off to where he might be. Every night for the past week, Charlie and I have scoured Dad's office. We broke into drawers, dissected files, ripped open boxes, even tried getting into his laptop. All unsuccessful in giving us anything that could help. I made the rounds at the tracks again, too, hitting them up while they were busy, just in case I might spot him in his usual place at the bar, or in his "lucky" seat. A man like my father gets around. I'm sure every bookie and other gambling addict at the tracks know his name.

Still nothing.

I can't stop panicking over how suspicious it all is—

the fact that nobody has seen him, that half the people I talk to won't even cop to knowing who he is...it's like they've been scared or bribed into silence. Or maybe marrying a Bellanti has made me paranoid.

Each evening I find myself going home later and later. I stayed over at the Abbott compound with my sisters last night, the three of us sleeping in my old room just like we used to. I just can't face Dante right now. I'd probably end up fucking him in front of the whole damned staff. When I left the office that day he bent me over the desk, it was clear by the look on Ruby's face that she had heard everything.

Maybe I'll take Ruby out to lunch one day, load her up with mimosas, and see if I can get her to spill all my husband's sins. In the meantime, I just want to ignore the dirtbag I'm married to. And save Livvie from a similar pathetic fate.

At least the staff members of Bellanti Vineyards like me. Dante has thus far put up zero resistance to the things I've been ordering for the employees, though Jessica says I'm pandering to them. I don't care. Happy staff means happy customers. Which means happy business. It's easy math. Plus, it's no less than our workers deserve.

"Morning," Livvie murmurs, padding into the kitchen in her pink pajamas.

"You're up early," I tell her. "Want me to make you some breakfast?"

She smiles. "I'm always up by six for the horses, and

I'm more than happy with my Pop Tarts, thank you very much. But I *will* steal some of that coffee."

I pour her a cup and we chat for a bit before she dashes upstairs to get her riding clothes on. Donovan slept in the guest room last night, since he refused to return to the Bellanti estate without me, so I make a quick stop at the barn to hug Livvie goodbye before heading back to Bellanti Vineyards.

"Thanks, Donovan," I say. "I appreciate you staying over."

"My pleasure," he says.

Staring out the window, I think about how quiet Livvie has been about Dad missing. I don't press too hard; just keep reassuring her that we'll find him soon. But whenever Charlie or I mention Dad coming home, Livvie's expression goes stony. I'm not sure she even wants him to be found. Which worries me. Growing up, we always tried to shield her from the worst of our dad's behavior—but I was in Italy for three years and Charlie moved out after she got married. Poor Livvie has been left to deal with Dad on her own, and all that shielding we tried to do hasn't been worth a shit. Maybe she thinks he's better off gone.

I'm tempted to stay another night. Livvie is absolutely vibrant with the three of us reunited, and I hate to lose that. But there's work to do at the winery today.

A few days ago, I went out on a limb and started expanding the upsell items on offer in the tasting room. First I approached Delores about selling some of her fruit cups and the signature peach wine the Alvarez family has been making for several generations. The Bellantis don't produce a sweet dessert wine, so it's the perfect complement to our selection.

I also had Donovan take me to a few local bakeries to sample the goods and ended up contracting with a French *viennoiserie* (basically a combination of bread bakery and pastry shop) to have an offering of croissants, fruit tarts, and other baked goods delivered to the tasting room early each morning. Not only am I promoting other businesses in town, but I'm endearing myself and Bellanti Vineyards to the advisory board at the chamber of commerce—they've always encouraged the wineries in Napa to work together and keep up the region's good reputation.

In the handful of days since starting the new upsells, sales have been up seven percent. I'm definitely not writing that off as a coincidence. The locals are happy, the winery visitors are happy, and our staff are happy too. Well, except for Jessica. Greg recreated her reaction to seeing the changed showroom and expanded offerings, nailing her pompous, indignant anger so well that I was almost in tears from laughing. She thinks my business practices are out of touch with the winery's demographic, that my bid to make employees happy by getting them needed equipment is a pointless waste of money. But all I see are smiles and open wallets, so who's really out of touch here? Just saying.

When I reach the tasting room, I find the parking lot overflowing. Making my way inside, I immediately catch Greg's gaze across the room. He looks equal parts harried and pleased and I can tell he's been running his ass off. The room is packed with milling guests, holding their wineglasses while they chat and peruse the nearly empty shelves of local goods. I tilt my head toward them with my brows raised and Greg gives me a thumbs-up.

The staff is attentively tending the tasting stations. From my spot near the entrance, I can see the fireplace is lit, the seating around it occupied; small groups chat near the windows where the sun is getting ready to set. In the back, nearly every table is full as staff bring out trays of bread and cheese and fresh fruit, including Delores's fruit cups.

My chest swells and I mentally high-five the staff. I go to the bar, forcing myself to walk and not run in triumph, and stash my purse under the counter. Leaning into Greg, I can't keep the smile off my face.

"Well, this is quite a development."

He nods. "We were slated to do inventory after the morning tasting, but people just kept coming in, so the doors stayed open. We've already restocked the bakery items twice and we're nearly sold out."

"Nice."

"Real nice. The only problem is, Mr. Bellanti needs the inventory done by tonight. Which means some of the staff is going to have to pull overtime now. I haven't told them yet."

I think it over. "Okay, so we'll offer bonus pay. And childcare reimbursement for anyone who needs it."

Greg shakes his head with a little smile. "I'll see if I can rustle up some volunteers."

I tend to guests while Greg makes his way through the employees. We have a handful of volunteers in no time, and I spend the rest of the day working in the tasting room.

Around six p.m., there's a lull at the bar, so I take the opportunity to restock some of the shelves and sweep up around the tables. That's when I notice a line forming at one of the registers. The crated display of wines there is nearly empty. People are gathered around it, whispering excitedly and grabbing multiple bottles. Curious which wine is drawing such attention, I'm about to go look when Dante appears at my side, his arm going around my waist.

"We're having dinner at the main house. Let's go."

I spy a flash of red over his shoulder and see Jessica has stomped her way inside. She rudely interrupts an employee who's assisting guests, pointing at something on her tablet.

"Things are a little busy here. I'll take a break when everyone else does."

Dante smirks. I assume he's about to pull rank. "Then I guess I came at the perfect time."

"What's that supposed to mean?" I ask.

Just then, the doors fly open as a parade of caterers enter pushing carts loaded with serving dishes and pitchers of water and a few bottles of Bellanti wine.

"It means I ordered a fine meal for the entire staff, which means you'll be taking your dinner with me now."

My mouth falls open at his latest bid to manipulate me, but I don't get a chance to say anything as Jessica clips over. "We have a problem, Dante. Did you realize the inventory hasn't been done yet, and your wife just authorized a *bonus* for employees to work overtime and finish it?"

"It'll get done." His expression is stony. "And you'll stay late to oversee it."

Her cheeks flush. "I'm not staying late just because—"

"Excuse us," Dante says acidly. "Oh, and make sure you email the inventory sheets over as soon as you're done with them."

Jessica says nothing, just watches with a jealous death-glare as Dante tightens his possessive grip on me and guides me out the door.

Back in the main house, we get to the dining room and find Armani and Marco working their way through the bread and wine. Dinner is brought out by the kitchen staff nearly the moment Dante and I are seated. The men start up a conversation, but I sit quietly and just listen. I don't want to get involved. It seems like every time I open my mouth around Dante, we end up in an argument, and I'm not up for it. Easier to play the obedient wife and just not participate.

Marco watches me over his wineglass, a twinkle of mischief in his eyes.

"I think a quiet Francesca is a dangerous Francesca. What's on your mind?"

I laugh. "Me? Dangerous? I'm not sure what Dante has been telling you, but I can guarantee it's not true."

He laughs and turns back to his food, but I guess it's enough to break the ice with me because Armani jumps in right after and says, "I bet she's thinking about how beautiful the showroom is now that she's brilliantly rearranged it. Maybe plotting what to do next."

Marco raises his glass. "Please, improve Dante next. His ego is intolerable lately."

I look between the brothers. "I'm not ready for a project of that size. I think I'll tackle something a little easier first."

The men—besides Dante, of course—laugh and toast our little banter.

Marco sits back in his chair. "I have to admit, it is nice to have a pretty woman at the dinner table again."

Armani and Dante shoot him a look. Ah, now here's an opening I want in on.

I take a sip of wine and look directly at Marco. "Again?" I ask innocently.

There's a pause as the brothers exchange a glance. Armani frowns at his youngest brother before putting on a tolerant smile, as if he's going to placate me despite really not wanting to.

"Our mother and sister were lost at sea when we were young."

My hand flies to cover my mouth. I wasn't expecting this kind of answer at all. "I'm so sorry, I had no—"

Armani waves away my condolences. "It was a long time ago. We've worked through it, though our father never did. It...changed him. He became—"

Dante sets his fork down hard on his plate. "My wife doesn't need to know the family sob story." He reaches into his breast pocket and pulls out his cell. It's vibrating gently.

"Like it or not, I'm part of the Bellanti family now," I say. I lean forward in my chair to address Armani quietly. "Really, I'd love to know as much about the family history as I can."

Armani seems to soften. He looks like he's about to speak again when Marco's cell lets out a muffled ping next to his plate. Marco grabs it up, earning him a scowl from Armani, but the frown freezes on his face as his own phone starts vibrating.

"Excuse me," Armani murmurs, turning away to look at his screen.

"What the fuck?" Dante pushes out of his chair, nearly toppling it. My heart sinks as the other men's expressions go tight.

Just then, my phone goes off too. I don't hesitate to pull it out of my pocket immediately and see what it is, but once I read the text from Greg, I wish I hadn't.

There are hundreds of thousands of dollars in inventory missing.

Someone fucked up. Bad.

We leave dinner on the table and rush to the tasting room. I can hear Jessica screaming as soon as we step inside. She's in the back with the employees, hollering at the top of her lungs. I only catch pieces of what's she's saying around the rush of blood in my ears.

"Liars...stealing from your employer...there *will* be legal consequences, for any and all of you involved, and you can be sure..."

Dante grabs Jessica by the arm and pulls her to the side, silencing her with a crushing look. Armani moves to one of the laptops and starts pulling up reports while Marco looks over his shoulder, lips pressed into a tense line.

I stand beside my husband as he begins, a bit more level-headedly, questioning the staff about what happened, thinly veiling his threats. They shuffle and look at the ground, intimidated by him, no doubt. But nobody has answers. Dante probably wouldn't believe anything they have to say, anyway.

"I think I figured it out," Armani says. "The wine wasn't...stolen, exactly."

"What the hell does that mean?" Dante asks. "Is it here, or is it not here?"

Armani brings the laptop over and shows him the screen. "It's not here. It was sold—at the wrong price. Our seven-hundred-fifty-dollar bottles are coming up at the thirty-five dollar peach wine price. The wines were labeled with this barcode here, but it rings up at thirty-five."

I can feel the blood drain from my face.

Dante taps the screen. "There are twenty bottles per case. How many were sold?"

"Forty-three cases."

Jessica steps forward and glares at me. "That's six hundred thousand dollars' worth of wine. Sold for thirty-thousand."

Dante nearly pulls the laptop from his brother's hand, but Armani moves away. "It had to be that someone put the wrong barcodes on the wine and didn't double-check how it rung up."

Jessica is still glaring at me. My heart starts to race. In the echoing silence, Greg clears his throat.

"I had brought up the point before that the crates of the cheaper wine looked very similar to the luxury wine. Perhaps that caused some confusion."

"*Confusion?*" Jessica cocks her head. "Someone *didn't do their job*." Stalking over to me, she pounces. "Weren't you the one who put the barcodes on the crates?"

My legs feel like they can't hold me. I look up at Dante by increments as my lips part and the words tumble out.

"Yes. I was in charge of labeling the bottles. I know they were correct, though."

I run the scenario through my mind. The thing is, I *did* double-check the labels. I *did* make sure they rang up at the right price. I triple-checked. But the look on my husband's face is so murderous, it will do no good to make excuses. And I'm beyond embarrassed that this is happening in front of the entire staff.

"Do you have any idea what you've done?" Jessica hisses.

Before I can answer, Dante grabs my arm and leads me out of the room—but not before I catch the gleeful, smug look on Jessica's face.

There's no doubt in my mind: that bitch is behind this. I know those were the right labels on the wine. I'd bet my life on it.

24

FRANKIE

I HAVE the lapels of my fluffiest feel-good bathrobe pulled up around my jaw, my body slouched into it like a personal blanket fort. I've been wrapped up in this old thing since leaving the tasting room in disgrace. Sitting on the edge of the massive tub in my private en suite watching hot water pour from the tap, I swirl in some dried lavender and expensive bath salts that claim to invoke "calm and peace."

The only thing that could possibly bring me calm and peace right now would be seeing Jessica getting her ass handed to her for the trick she pulled.

I don't know how she managed to get away with switching up the barcodes, but I'm one-hundred-percent confident that she's behind this fiasco. Being grounded in that theory isn't stopping me from feeling guilty and ashamed, though. I've been continually second-guessing myself, worried I may have been the culprit after all. What if I really did screw up this badly?

Hundreds of thousands of dollars have been lost to this one mistake, and if I really am to blame...Dante will never let me set foot inside the business again. Even if he did, the staff will have lost all respect for me anyway. Which means I'll be trapped inside this mausoleum of a house, alone, with nothing to do to pass the time. Slowly dying here, useless and stagnant.

I dump more bath salts into the water. No. I'm not going to let that happen to me. It's clear as day that Jessica staged this whole thing to drive a wedge between me and Dante—and fuck up my career while she was at it —and she's going to come clean, one way or another. I just need to figure out a way to strong-arm her into admitting that she set me up.

The tub is full. I turn off the water and am just about to slip out of my robe when I hear the lock on my bedroom door snick. The back of my neck tingles even as the hint of masculine vetiver cologne tells me Dante has come in. Without knocking, of course.

He's just the kind of asshole to saunter in here and lecture me about the mistake I supposedly made. I feel him coming toward me, hear his footsteps pause just inside the bathroom. He's watching me. Probably leaning against the door frame, pouting, arms crossed.

I keep my back to him, stirring the water, ignoring him on purpose as I inhale the scent of lavender. Resentment floods my body. I want him to leave. The guilt is enough of a punishment on its own. He doesn't need to bust in here just to make me feel worse.

Finally, I can't take it. I give a cursory glance behind

me. Maybe if I let him get it out of his system now, he'll leave so I can slide into the tub.

"What do you want?" The words snap from my lips.

One corner of his hard lips tugs up. It's not quite a sneer, but close enough.

"I have a question for you, Francesca. There's something I want to know."

"O-kay." I gesture impatiently for him to go ahead.

"How..." He takes a step closer. "The *hell*..." Another step, making my heart skip. "Are you going to make up for this catastrophic loss to my winery?" And then one more.

He's now standing right in front of me, glaring down as if he actually expects me to respond to that.

"You lost way more than money the day you hired Jessica," I tell him. "Why don't you scrutinize her assets and ask her how *she's* going to pay?"

"Seriously, Francesca."

Getting to my feet, I cross my arms to hold my anger back. "I *am* being serious. I don't know how, but she's behind this. I used the correct barcodes. I triple-checked everything."

He scoffs. "Just because you don't like someone doesn't mean you get to blame them when shit goes wrong."

"Thank you for those words of *wisdom*, oh great and noble master," I say, my voice dripping sarcasm.

I wish he was standing closer to the window. I'd push him out so I can take my damn bath.

Before I can blink, Dante is on me. He presses my arms to my sides and drives me back against the wall. My heart pounds, fury heating my skin even as tingles of desire race over me.

His hand finds my throat, pressing there firmly as he jacks my chin up, forcing me to look at him. "I *am* your master."

I'm too angry to be afraid. "You and your ego can fuck directly off. I've had more than enough of your machismo bullshit."

I wiggle against him, knowing full well that he's not about to let me go.

Dante smiles before he dips his head, his lips finding my ear. His warm breath ghosts over the delicate skin, sending shivers through my body. His husky voice is hard and unfeeling.

"And yet...you never tell me no, do you? You never put a stop to it. You *want it*. Every single time."

Shame heats my cheeks. My lack of backtalk is response enough to egg him on.

"If I put my hand between your legs right now, I'll find you soaking wet, won't I? Even though you hate me." He smiles, drawing a slow breath, and my nipples perk tight against the soft fabric of my robe. "That's pretty fucked up, Francesca."

"Don't call me that!" I push him just enough to drive his chest back from mine, but it only makes him look at me like a hungry wildcat ready to pounce. I'm already imagining the feel of his warm, smooth, naked skin on mine. His fingers pulling at my nipples and palming my breasts as he roughly works his way down my body.

Without another word, he flings me over his shoulder

and carries me out of the bathroom, then tosses me onto the bed. He's on top of me in an instant, pulling at the belt of my robe and spreading the sides open. I push at him, twist and turn, but it's no use. My desire gets stronger and more demanding even as I tell myself that I don't want this. That I won't allow him to use me this way.

My protests sound hollow, even as I think them, so I don't dare give them voice. Because he's right: I don't mean it. I *do* want him to use me this way. Over and over and over again.

Dante shrugs out of his shirt. I'm desperate to see his broad, bare chest and run my hands over his pecs, the hard ridges of his abs. Curling my fingers into my palms, I struggle to resist. Now he's on the bed straddling me, clamping his thighs around my hips. My robe is wide open, my breasts and belly bare to his view. He rakes my body with a starving look and I swear I could orgasm just from the appreciation and want in his expression.

Why is he looking at me like I'm the best fucking thing he's ever seen? He's obviously playing me to get what he wants. Feeding my undeniable lust for him so he can turn me into his personal sex kitten. Pulling my body up until I'm in a sitting position, Dante pulls the robe from my arms, tossing it away. Then, with one hand, he unfastens his pants and kicks them off.

My heart flips to see he's commando and the best part of him is full, thick, and jutting out proudly. I lick my lips as the ache between my legs kicks up another notch. My mind spins like I'm drunk, and my inhibitions are completely gone. He can do anything he wants to me and I'd welcome it with open arms...and legs.

Fuck, this has to stop. I think it with complete clarity. He always wins. *Always.*

The fight goes out of me and I go limp. He takes my wrists in his hands, but I don't resist. I don't move a single finger. I just...lay there. Passive. He frowns, then goes still as well.

"You're just going to let me win?"

Ah. So this *is* a game to him. Bastard.

It's *all* a game to him. My life. My career. My feelings. Everything.

"You won the moment my father agreed to this stupid marriage contract. I'm tired of fighting you, Dante. And I'm tired of trying to prove myself to you. I don't care anymore. Do what you want."

His jaw works back and forth. Turning my head, I look away and wait to see what he'll do next. A small part of me hopes he'll leave. But then he stretches out fully on top of me, his hard cock wedged between my thighs. Instinctively, my hips strain to meet his, but I stop myself.

Dante glares down at me, and I glare back.

"Tell me I'm the only one," he commands.

It might be the last thing I was expecting him to say. "What? I don't—"

"Tell me I'm the only man you want. Just say it!"

Fine. What's his deal? "You're the only man I want."

He juts his hips down, his cock sliding between my

pussy lips. I can only spread my legs enough to allow him the smallest access, but it's enough. Oh, hell, it's enough.

"Again," he says.

"You're the only. Man. I want." I tease out the words, locking eyes with him.

"Again."

He makes me say it over and over, that I want him, that I need him, only him, his hands, his mouth, his cock. As I repeat the words like a mantra, I sink into the pleasure, losing myself in the all-consuming way that's become all too familiar with this man. He kisses his way down my body, pulling a nipple into his hot mouth and pressing it with his lips. My fingers dig into his hair as he kisses his way down over my belly, leaving shivers behind. I'm desperate for him to touch between my legs. His lips and his fingers meet there at the same time and I spread my thighs wide for him.

"Fuck yes. Dante. I need you," I pant.

"Again."

Closing my eyes, I roll my head back. I'll say anything he wants if it means I get to come.

"I need you."

His fingers part me, his tongue darting straight to the most desperate spot. I can hardly hold still as he feasts on my clit and traces my sensitive inner lips with his fingers. I'm swollen and tingling and holding his head tight as I ride his fingers, his tongue, feeling the wetness dripping out of me as he laps it up. It's so good I can hardly breathe, moaning so loud I'm sure everyone in the house can hear me. I'm close...so close...almost there...oh, yes, oh God...

My eyes sting with sudden tears, my body useless to fight as I reach the point of no turning back.

"Say it!"

His voice rips through my ears just as I start to come, and I gasp out, "I love you."

The shock of what just came out of my mouth is lost as my orgasm overtakes me in a hot rush. My pussy is pulsing with deep contractions when Dante slams his cock into me and rides me hard, pressing me into the bed so the entire frame shakes against the floor. My release never quite died away—it builds again with each thrust, flaming hotter...hotter...

Dante groans and ruts two hard, quick thrusts into my greedy body. I come again with a forceful flash of pleasure that makes stars burst behind my eyes.

He rolls off me, one arm flung over my chest. I'm staring up at the ceiling, trying to catch my breath, when the reality of what I just said creeps to the forefront of my mind.

Oh. God. Why the *hell* did I say that? He most definitely didn't tell me to.

I turn my head to the side and catch his gaze. There's something open and raw on his face, just beneath the surface, an expression I can't fully comprehend because it doesn't match the man. He looks...vulnerable. For a moment, I think he's about to say something. Or maybe pull me into his arms and stay with me.

But then he slips off the bed, wordlessly gathering his clothes, leaving me shivering without his warmth. I close my eyes and listen to the quiet sounds of him dressing.

His feet pad softly across the carpet.

I don't watch him leave.

25

FRANKIE

It's hard to sleep when your thoughts are screaming at you all night long.

Unfortunately, my body clock is firmly set to wake me at sunrise, so now I'm lying in bed with my eyes wide open and literally no reason to get up. The tasting room is closed on Mondays anyway, so regardless of my questionable employment status, I have to find a way to occupy my entire day.

I haven't felt depressed like this in a long time. Maybe ever.

Not just over the inventory debacle, or the fact that Jessica seems to have gotten away with blaming it on me —but because my husband also came inside me again last night. I'm on a losing streak right now, and I'm angry at myself for not doing more to prevent some of it.

Granted, there is little I could have done to stop Jessica. But I *can* control my pregnancy risk. Starting now.

Dante might want an heir, but he can't actually force me to give him one. Because even with him not using condoms, there are plenty of other birth control methods out there. Hell, I started taking the pill when I was sixteen, and I'm happy to go back on it—I just haven't gotten around to having my prescription updated since I returned from Italy, which has left me vulnerable. Damn it. I need to add "make appointment with OBGYN" to my mental to-do list.

In fact, I'll call today.

Hand straying over my abdomen, I think about the possibility of a baby growing there already. God, please not yet. Not when my life is such a shitshow. I'm not ready for a baby. *We're* not ready for a baby.

What would having a child with Dante even be like? He's so controlling and stone-faced most of the time, I can't honestly imagine him as a father. Especially when he's made it clear that he views offspring as "heirs" rather than actual children. But maybe having a kid would change him in ways I can't imagine. Maybe he'd find a softer side of himself, patient and loving and attentive.

Or maybe he'd just be his usual cold, indifferent self, dumping our child off on a series of nannies and private boarding schools while he runs his empire.

The last thing I want to do is bring a child into this world as a guinea pig.

Reaching for my phone, I type my old gynecologist's name into Google to get her number. Just then, a message from Charlie pops up. *How fast can you get here?*

My heart begins a furious pace at what's prompting a question like that. 20 *min or so? What's wrong?*

Please don't let it be Livvie.

There's a pause and I almost call my sister, but another text comes through. *Dad's home.*

"Oh, fuck." I read those two words again. "Shit."

I can't move him by myself and I need you to see something. Hurry.

Can't move him? What the hell is going on over there? Bursting from the bed, I throw on a pair of leggings and a tee shirt, slip into my sandals, and hurry out the door. I don't even bother brushing my teeth, I'm so anxious to get over to Dad's.

Downstairs, I swerve into the small hallway closet where the keys are kept and grab the set to my little red convertible. Dante only returned them to me recently, and I'm probably about to make him regret that decision. But maybe if I can get back soon enough, nobody will even know I was gone.

I pull the Jaguar out of the garage and speed down the long driveway, kicking up rocks under the tires. I'm just past the Bellanti gates when my cell rings.

The sound makes me jump. It has to be Dante. His spidey senses probably went off the second I crossed over the property line, and now he's going to chew me out.

Not that I care. I'm a grown-ass adult and this is a family emergency. He can fight me.

I accept the call and hit the speakerphone button, realizing only too late that I don't recognize the number on the screen. Is it something to do with Dad? The hospital? I answer hesitantly, my adrenaline surging.

"Hello?"

"Frankie! Hey, babe, it's—"

Fuck. Rico.

I end the call and throw the phone onto the floorboard, not caring if it breaks. The sound of the caller's voice echoes in my head, and I grip the wheel harder.

This is not what I need right now. Or ever.

My throat constricts. Why is my life such a fucking mess? The little disasters keep piling on and piling on and I'm not sure how much more I can take.

Focusing on the road, I drive as fast as I dare to the Abbott compound, even though the last thing I need right now is another run-in with a cop. Guess I'll take my chances.

When I get to the house, the car's barely in park before I run up to the door. Charlie meets me there. "Tell me," I pant out breathlessly. "And where's Livvie?"

"Shh, she's fine. She's at school," Charlie says. "I haven't told her he's back yet."

"Where is he?"

My sister's eyes flick from side to side, as if someone might be lurking on our property eavesdropping. She ushers me into the house and locks the door, keeping her voice low.

"About a half an hour ago, some car drove up and rolled him out of the back. A black car, I don't know what kind, I was in the front room with my paints."

"Is he injured?" I ask, whispering.

Charlie shakes her head. "I don't know. He had a piece of paper pinned to his shirt with a very high number written on it. One million."

"Dollars?" I gasp. "Fuck. What did he do this time?"

"I don't know. He's not talking. Maybe you can get something out of him. He's either been on a serious bender or else they drugged him, because he can't seem to focus. I brought water and saltines to him in the den, but he might be passed out again."

We tiptoe down the hallway and peek into the den. I'm expecting to see Dad asleep on the couch, or maybe the floor. What I'm *not* expecting to see is him perched on the edge of the ottoman with one of our grandmother's big antique vases in his hands, staring into it bleakly with his mouth open.

"Dad, no!"

I run toward him, but it's too late. He retches into the vase, his fingers gripping the sides as he heaves.

"Fuck, Dad," Charlie says. "That's the one with a crack in it."

Yes, it is. And now it's leaking onto both him and the floor.

"I'll get a towel and some cleaner," I tell my sister.

She sighs. "God, this is like senior prom all over again."

"And Livvie's fifteenth birthday party," I add.

"And that time we—"

Dad heaves again and reaches a hand out as if he's trying to swat at us. I dart into the kitchen and grab a few dish towels, another bottle of water, and some Lysol.

When I get back, Dad is wiping his mouth with the back of his hand.

"Iss gonna be okay," he tells us, slurring his words. "We'll juss...sell off the rest of the horses."

Livvie's horses? Oh, *hell no*. That is it. I am DONE with the men in my life.

I drop the supplies in my arms, march over to him, and drag him down by the front of his shirt until he's on the floor on one knee. His eyes flash with anger as he tries to grab me.

"Dad—" Charlie starts.

"Lemme go," he mumbles.

I slap him. Hard, across the face. The sound of it reverberates through the room, the sting of it jolting through my palm and up my arm, straight to my heart.

"Enough," I hiss. "You're not selling Livvie's horses, or anything else. Look at me."

He refuses, keeping his eyes on the floor. It's clear he's still not feeling well, sweat beading at his temples, his skin pale and the broken blood vessels visible on his cheeks and nose. I can't bring myself to feel sorry for him, though. Something inside me has come unleashed.

Digging my fingers into his shirt, I pull violently, trying to get him to look up. He's a big man, more than capable on a good day of holding me off. But he's fucked up and weak and I'm very, very pissed.

"I said *look at me*, Dad!"

A soft hand touches my shoulder. I smell Charlie's perfume. Her fingers curl over my shoulder and she pulls back, taking me with her. But I won't relent. I shrug her off and cross my arms, glaring down at my father on the floor.

"Who killed Enzo Bellanti?" I demand.

Behind me, Charlie gasps.

"The hell should I know?" he says.

I'm out of patience. Moving eye level with him, I speak again, slowly and clearly. "Who. Killed. Enzo. Bellanti."

Dad just smiles. His lower lip has a scab down the center, as if it had been split and healed up some. If he smiles any wider, it'll probably bust open again. He doesn't answer, so I press a finger to the scab. He sucks in a breath.

"I asked you a question."

"I'm warning you, Frankie," he says.

"You have nothing to threaten me with. Do you understand that? You're not a threat. Not a parent. And certainly not someone I give a shit about. What you are is a *source of information* and you're either going to tell me what I need to know, or I'll let my husband get it out of you."

Beside me, Charlie shifts. "And mine. And trust me, he won't be as gentle as Frankie."

Dad squints, his jaw working just enough that I know he fully comprehends the meaning of what we just said.

"You married me off into the mob, Dad. You think I won't use that to my advantage?" I prod. "Who tampered with that car? *Give me the fucking name.*"

I'm breathing hard, barely able to contain my rage.

"Fine," I say with a fake smile. "I'm calling Dante. By

the way, have you seen the underground wine cellars the Bellantis have? They're huge. And dark. And cold. It's probably really easy to get lost down there. I doubt you'd even be able to hear anyone yelling for help."

I pull out my phone, and my dad suddenly yells, "Wait!"

He motions me closer. I consider that maybe he's going to try to strangle me as I lower onto my haunches and put my ear to his lips. Charlie must be considering that, too, because she's got a death grip on me as if she can singlehandedly pull me up from the lion's den.

Sighing deeply, he whispers a name. Then he pulls back, brows arching as if to gauge my reaction. He's breathing hard, still visibly sweating. It looks like he might vomit again.

I cross to the mantel to grab another vase. This one's undamaged.

Handing it to him, I say, "Try not to choke to death."

Taking my sister's arm, I guide her out into the sunshine. We leave Dad back in the den with his vase and his misery. Alone.

DANTE

WHERE THE HELL does she think she's going?

I lower my coffee mug mid-sip and watch from my office balcony as my wife flies down the driveway in her little red Jag. She must have managed to get around Donovan somehow—I should send him after her. Or go get her myself. There's a tracker on her car for situations like this, so it wouldn't take long to find her.

And since our handover deal with the Bruno clan isn't going as smoothly as I'd anticipated, I can't be too careful. One misstep could mean trouble, and I'd never forgive myself if Francesca was at the receiving end. I'm not about to let that happen. My line of work is exactly why, between her phone and her car, I know where she is at all times. Just in case.

Phone in hand, I'm about to call Donovan, but something stops me. I'm not sure what it is...but I can't think back on last night without feeling...something. The look in her eyes, the way she just...gave in. Like all the fight suddenly went out of her. It got to me. I can't help worrying that I broke something important in her—something that made her important to me.

I enjoy her spirit, and the way she battles me feeds my need to be challenged. Maybe I've become addicted to our intense tug-of-wars. What if I stripped that away, and now it's lost for good? My wife has confounded me at every turn, and at this point I have no idea how to act, what to say or do.

The French doors behind me open and Armani strolls onto the balcony.

"Figured you'd be out here," he says.

I give him a once-over, noticing he's dressed unusually casually even for his day off. Following in the footsteps of our late father, we both take off the second Monday of every month. It was a concession he made to our mother early on in their marriage, a promise he made (and kept) to ensure that at least one day a month revolved around her and not his work.

Not that "day off" means the same thing to me or Armani that it did to Dad. Case in point: my brother has a tablet in one hand, and the outline of his cell phone presses against his pocket. Even though he's in Dockers and a checked button-down—hell, he even left the top few buttons undone—I know he'll be working all day. Albeit from the comfort of a recliner or with a bottle of wine uncorked in front of him, but still. He's a workaholic. Both of us are.

Marco is the only Bellanti who was ever born without

an iron work ethic, and to be honest, sometimes I envy him.

"This better be good," I say to Armani, making a big show of slurping my coffee. "It's my day off."

He knows I'm joking. "What the hell is a day off?" he jokes back.

"Talk to me."

He flips the case to the tablet open. My gut tenses, as if sensing bad news.

"So I was looking into the sales records again—"

I frown. "Is this about the inventory fuckup?"

"Yeah. Funny story. See, I went into the stockroom to check out the labels on the crates of the Elite Reserve cabs. Know what's crazy? They were the right labels."

My frown deepens. "How's that possible? They rang up wrong."

Armani nods. "That they did. Seemed to me a little more detective work was called for."

"Spit it out, man." I'm rapidly losing patience.

My brother starts pacing, talking with his hands, drawing his story out just to push my buttons. Because that's what brothers are for. "So I ask myself, 'If the labels are correct, how can they be scanning at the wrong price?' That's not a labeling issue. That's a *software* issue."

I'm starting to pick up what he's putting down. "Okay. Sure. But the program doesn't make edits by itself. Someone would've had to go in and change the barcode assignment in the program..."

"Exactly! It's the only way you could scan the right

label and get the wrong price. Someone edited the inventory field so that *that* barcode would come up as a thirty-five-dollar item." He turns at the end of the balcony and paces back toward me. "So I looked up the timestamp on the sales receipts and pinpointed the timeframe when the change took place."

I grab the tablet out of his hand. "Show me."

Leaning over, he taps the screen, navigating to the inventory management module. A few more taps and I can see the dates when all the product labels were scanned in.

"Frankie scanned in the labels here. See? Correct vintage, correct price. Two days of sales corroborate that the wines in question were labeled correctly." He pegs me with a stare. "Interestingly enough, the next person to log into the software was *Jessica*. And the activity log shows she was the only person who signed in that day."

Taking the tablet from my brother, I go through the evidence page by page. The trail is there, clear to see. The Elite Reserve price dropped on the same day that Jessica had her hands in the software, and no one has logged in since—until Armani did today.

"Jessica did this. She was responsible," I growl. "Not Francesca."

I go silent, battling my inner rage. Armani takes the tablet back and slowly closes the case, not taking his eyes off me.

"What?" I snap, nearly throwing my coffee mug over the balcony just so I can hear it smash on the ground below.

He rolls his eyes. "That feeling you're having right now? It's called shame. I saw the look on your face when you went to talk to Francesca last night—you need to make it right with her. She's better than you deserve."

"Get the fuck off my balcony."

Armani smiles, backing away with his hands up. "It'll be my balcony when you die childless and alone, brother."

I'm not going to dignify that with a response. "Goodbye, Armani."

"You're welcome, Dante." He goes back inside, shutting the balcony doors behind him.

I don't linger over the rest of my coffee, finishing it in a hurry and scrubbing my face with my hands. This is a lot of shit to process, but I know I don't have time to mull it over.

Jessica must be dealt with.

The worst part is, Francesca tried to tell me she was a problem, and I thought it was jealousy talking. Hell, that's not completely true. I've always known Jessica was a loose wire, but I've been too busy to rein her in. And look what happened. This mistake is mine.

I go inside and send her a text. *Meet me at the house. My wife isn't home.* That'll bring her running.

When her car pulls up outside, tires crunching on the driveway, I go downstairs to confront her. I'm fixing my right cuff as I descend, one slow step at a time. I'm not in a hurry to see her, or the cock-hungry look on her face. I've been pissed at her before, but never like this.

"Dante," she says eagerly.

239

"Jessica."

I reach her, and just like I presumed, she's dressed like she's expecting us to fuck. She's in a skin-tight blue dress, her cleavage heaving over the neckline, and her heels are four inches tall. She's on me in a flash, her hands running up and down my arms as she steps into me. Her breasts press against my chest, her hot breath in my ear.

"I'm so glad you texted—"

Removing myself from her octopus arms, I push her away and ground her with a stare.

"You changed the pricing on the barcodes."

Her eyes narrow as if she's confused. "What? No. I certainly did not."

"Armani tracked your software logins. You're the only one besides my wife who accessed inventory management before the Elite Reserve price got fucked up."

Jessica grips her clutch with both hands, as if it can shield her from my wrath.

"There must be a misunderstanding. I don't know anything about that. I don't even know *how* to do that."

I flash her a cold smile. "But you did log in?"

Her mouth opens, closes. "I...yes, I did log in. I was adding new inventory to the system—the dessert wines we just got in. That's all I did."

"Really? Huh. That's interesting. Because I have sales receipts reflecting the correct price *before* you logged in, and receipts reflecting the incorrect price *after* you logged in. Which is fascinating. Because nobody else used the program. It's almost as if...it *had* to be you."

A moment passes. My eyes drill into hers.

She drops her eyes to the floor. "Okay. Fine. I made changes to some of the barcode descriptions. I was trying to update the system with the dessert wine, but something happened, and...I guess I accidentally overwrote the Elite Reserve info. I couldn't figure out how to undo it. I swear I didn't realize what happened until it was too late, Dante. It was an honest mistake."

I nod, letting out a long breath, think carefully about what to say next. There's a thunderstorm inside me right now and if I don't temper myself, I'm going to rain down on this bitch. "I believe you."

Jessica's shoulders sag with relief. "I just—"

"But I also believe you should have owned up to your mistake instead of trying to use it to break up my marriage."

She smiles, as if I've just made some kind of joke. "Dante, you can't be serious—"

"You're fired," I tell her flatly. "So pack up your things from the office, get the fuck out of my life, and stay away from Francesca."

The color drains from her face. "Dante, we can talk about this."

"*We're done.*" I lower my voice, leaning in menacingly. "And if I were you, I'd say my prayers real hard tonight. Because I could have easily arranged for you to not make it home in one piece."

Her chin juts but she doesn't say anything else before stomping out the door in a rage. The sound of her footsteps is loud on the stone driveway until the roar of an engine overtakes it. I reach the doorway and see Francesca getting out of the Jag just as Jessica reaches her own car.

The two women pause just long enough to exchange words. My wife's expression changes just a touch, but I can't hear what Jessica's saying to her.

Francesca storms toward the house, her fists clenched —and I get the impression there's a lot more going on than just anger over seeing Jessica here. Either way, I can tell my wife is geared up for battle. And I'm very much looking forward to this fight.

27

FRANKIE

Dante watches me as I storm toward the house and head straight for him, daggers in my eyes. But by the time I get to the door, he's already heading upstairs, his back to me, without a lick of acknowledgement. The bastard's not getting away from me that easily.

I fling my purse onto the entry table with all my might, kick off my shoes, and stalk up the stairs after him.

"We need to talk!" I shout, but he just keeps walking like the jerk that he is.

I was gone for a few hours dealing with a legitimate family crisis, and he filled the time with a fucking booty call. My emotions are over the top right now, trapped inside me, making me tremble from head to toe. Dealing with my father drained me, and having Jessica mean-girl me in the driveway just now has pushed me over the edge.

At the top of the stairs, I hear the click of Dante's home office door shutting. Does he think that's going to keep me out? I'll break down the goddamn door if I have to.

But when I try the knob, it's unlocked. I stride into the room, and see him standing out on the balcony. Good. The whole vineyard can listen to me. I'm ready to go to war.

Flinging the French doors open, I stalk over to Dante until he's pushed back against the wrought iron balustrade.

Then I tell him, in flawless Italian, *"I'm not responsible for the mix up with the wine barcodes. I didn't fuck up. And not only did I not fuck up, but even with the sales fiasco, I've increased revenue* seven percent *since I started working in the tasting room."*

Dante looks at me, shaking his head slowly, as if I'm trying to pull a fast one on him.

"Oh, I'm sorry, did I neglect to mention that I'm fluent in Italian?" I say sarcastically. "That's something you probably would have liked to know before now, huh? Too bad you didn't make the effort to find out."

"Francesca—"

"It's *Frankie*, dammit, and I'm not done yet."

I switch back to Italian, just because I'm on a roll, and because yelling always sounds so much better in a Romance language.

"What was I saying? Seven percent? That's right. You know how I did that? By rearranging your main attraction, increasing flow through the tasting room, making the space more comfortable for guests, and expanding the upsell offerings with baked goods and crafts by local arti-

sans that visitors are snapping up at a record pace. But that's not all.

"I've gotten your business in good with Napa's chamber of commerce, established better relationships with shops and producers here in town, and I'm actively making Bellanti Vineyards a go-to destination for every wine tour and travel guide who comes through, not to mention sending pamphlets and gift baskets to the highest rated professional wedding planners in all fifty-eight counties, though I'll be expanding to other states as soon as it's viable.

"And, oh yeah, in my spare time I'm finalizing the blend that will utilize your castoff grapes and the Abbott Canaiolos in order to solve your uneven bottling numbers. Wasn't that the whole reason you wanted the Abbott vineyard to begin with?"

"Frankie—"

I'm nearly out of breath, but I cut him off anyway. *"AND, on top of all that, I solved your father's murder."*

I tell him the man's name, then switch back to English just to say, "Fuck you, Dante Bellanti."

Finally finished, I stand there in the late morning sun, panting slightly as the breeze ruffles my hair and cools my rage. Dante's just staring at me, as if he's never seen me before. Maybe he hasn't.

He lifts his arms and starts giving me the slow clap. Fuck this.

Scowling, I turn to go. Before I reach the French doors, he comes up behind me and grabs my wrist. Whipping around to glower at him, I yank my hand away. "Don't even—"

"I'm fucking impressed," he says.

Cocking my head, I gesture at him for more.

"You're off the hook for the wine labels," he adds. "Jessica confessed. I fired her."

I wait in case there's a punch line. I suppose gloating would be bad form at this point.

"Okay," I say slowly. "Did you hear what I said before? About your father?"

His face does that thing where every shred of emotion disappears. He's unreadable.

"Dante?"

"I heard you."

"So...?"

He digs his phone from his pocket and brushes past me into the office.

"So I have work to do. Make sure your sister has everything prepared for the First Press event tomorrow. And Frankie"—he looks back at me—"no more surprises."

FRANKIE

TODAY'S THE BIG DAY. Nothing can go wrong.

But considering the way that life here at Bellanti Vineyards has been going lately, that might be a bit of a longshot.

Charlie's been working on putting together the First Press event behind the scenes, doing what she does best, and pulling out all the stops so it'll be picture-perfect. My idea was the impetus for this whole thing, but to Marco's credit, he immediately latched onto the concept and ran with it. I guess because to him, it sounded a lot like throwing a huge party. As for Dante, he just signed on the dotted lines—with Armani's enthusiastic support, of course.

First Press will officially commemorate the first batches of Bellanti *and* Abbott grapes going into the winepress. After countless hours of research and debate and calculation, Dante, Marco, and I were finally able to come up with what we believe will be the perfect blend of Bellanti Sangiovese grapes and Abbott Canaiolo grapes. We're going to produce a spectacular Chianti, mark my words. And what better way to celebrate the marriage of the Bellanti and Abbott wineries than by launching a new annual tradition?

The media will be in attendance, the entire staff will be on hand, and the limited number of tickets we offered to the public sold out almost immediately. Close business associates and our local trade partners were invited, of course, and whomever the Bellantis had on their guest list. We're expecting to host about two hundred guests total. Basically the huge party Marco wanted, except this party is a combination press conference and exclusive wine tasting all in one.

Attendees will get a first taste of the previous year's harvest, along with outrageously expensive hors d'oeuvres from a catering company that Charlie swears by and special treats created by our friends at the *viennoiserie* just for the event. Then we'll have music and dancing to end the night.

Fates willing, First Press will be held every year. But in order to cement its permanent placement on the Bellanti calendar of events, it's imperative that we get off on the right foot today. So, yeah. No pressure. Beyond the initial idea, I haven't actually had a lot to do with the planning. That's my sister's department, and I'm both excited and anxious to see what she's arranged.

"Frankie."

Dante appears in the doorway of my bedroom as I'm putting my earrings in. I don't acknowledge him right away and he steps inside, taking up space in that way he has. I can't help but look. I glance, then look again and soak him up.

His suit is perfectly cut and accentuates all his strong, long lines. It's a three-piece sharkskin in deep charcoal with a light gray shirt and tie interwoven with pale yellow threads. Glancing down at myself, I'm astounded to realize that we...match. We didn't plan to. We certainly didn't talk about it ahead of time. But here we are.

"We're matching. A little bit, anyway," I say as I attempt to clasp my necklace. I'm having a hard time taking my eyes off him.

He comes up behind me, hands on my hips. I go completely still. His breath is warm on the back of my neck, and I shiver as he runs his hands up my sides before bringing them to my hands. He takes the necklace ends from my fingers and gently works the clasp.

"Yellow suits you," he says, smoothing the chain along the back of my neck, his touch trailing over my bare shoulders.

"Thank you."

His warmth is suddenly gone, and I realize he's stepped away. Looking at myself in the mirror, I fuss with my updo. Curls have already fallen into tendrils around my face. I leave them.

My pale-yellow pleated gown has a plunging yet tastefully narrow neckline, an empire waist, and a long skirt that brushes the tops of my heels. It's magical, reminiscent of a sunbeam...and it was egregiously expensive. But the moment I saw it, I knew it was the one—and now that I'm wearing it, I feel like a goddess. It's almost enough to take the sting of my problems away. Temporarily, at least.

Dante leans toward me and brings his mouth close to my ear. "Time to go."

I turn toward his voice, my lips nearly brushing his. We stare at each other a moment before he pulls away with a shadow of a grin and guides me out the door with his hand on the dip of my back.

The press conference is first. Media people are already assembled and waiting inside a white tent set up near the mouth of the vineyard. I take a glass of chardonnay from a tray that one of the waiters is revolving through the room with and hold it with both hands as Dante, Marco, and Armani gather behind a duo of microphones and face the waiting press.

Marco takes center and addresses the crowd. "Welcome to Bellanti Vineyards."

I wander just outside the tent while the Bellanti men talk, and take a moment to survey what my sister has created. The grounds are incredible. Little lights hang everywhere, the rows of bentwood chairs and long picnic tables perfectly arranged. Chandeliers hang from tree branches overhead, while topiaries grace the walkways between tables. She chose shades of blush pink, white, and pale green, giving a fresh, elegant look.

I spy Charlie and Livvie near the mini bar and give a little wave. Charlie winks and continues chatting with Livvie—probably lecturing her on not trying to sneak wine like she did at my wedding reception. Guests have started to arrive, and the beautiful space is beginning to fill up nicely. There are a lot of familiar faces, including Candi who I wave to, and Mrs. Alvarez who whipped up special fruit cups just for this event.

My phone rings from inside my clutch. I take it out and glance at the screen but don't recognize the number, so I don't answer. Both of my sisters are here. There's no one else I care about right now.

Before long, Dante and his brothers step out of the tent and into the sunshine. The press disperses to make their rounds while my husband heads straight for me. My heart flutters as he approaches, my body aching for contact.

"I want to keep you close today," he says, slipping my hand into the crook of his elbow.

"Are you going soft on me, dear husband?"

"Not at all. But it's my job to keep you out of trouble."

Pressing a hand to my chest in mock offense, I tease, "Are you saying you don't want me stripping down to my lingerie in front of your guests again?"

He quirks a brow. "Are you wearing any?"

I smile at a couple as they walk past us, then drop my voice. "Nope."

He clears his throat, but not before I hear a little groan escape him.

Just then, I see Charlie crook a finger at us from across the lawn.

Dante steers me toward her. "It's time to give everyone what they came for."

We join Marco and Armani at the entrance to the vineyard. Two workers roll out one of the old wooden grape presses first used by the Bellanti family when they started the winery. They set up the grape press on a platform, where everyone can see it. The platform holds two slat buckets: one containing grapes from Abbott vines, and one with Bellanti grapes.

The media people assemble around us, flashes going off, phone cameras clicking as Dante and I each pick up a cluster of our respective family's grapes and hold them up for show before putting them into the old press.

Armani gestures to the press with a flourish. "Let today mark the marriage of two great wineries. This union brings promise to the future of Bellanti winemaking, and the creation of unique blends that will be celebrated on this day, at the annual First Press event."

Now it's Marco's job to turn the crank on the press. When a stream of grape juice starts pouring out into a bucket, the crowd cheers and applauds, whooping and whistling. I feel light all of a sudden. Happy, even. As if we really have done something remarkable.

The wine flows, the buffet opens, and guests sip, nibble, and mill around, having a wonderful time. Dante and I make our way from table to table, talking and laughing with our guests as they enjoy their meals and the delicious vintages on offer. A band begins setting up at the gazebo under the trees, and I know the guests will be dancing well into the evening.

I'm on my third glass of wine but I don't know what's making me feel better: the wine, or the way Dante hasn't stopped touching me since we pressed the grapes. If I move too far out of his orbit, he pulls me back in. He keeps a hand on my lower back if he has to turn away to speak with someone, and he links his arm through mine as we walk through the crowd.

Music begins playing quietly as we finally sit with Marco and Armani to eat. The late afternoon sun has dropped low by the time we finish with dessert. Then the tables are cleared, and more wine is brought around. Dante takes my hand and pulls me to my feet, then spins me out onto the dance floor.

And he's smiling.

This feels like the wedding reception I wanted to have.

Both of us are lighter today, moving more easily in concert with each other, like a real couple. We seem almost happy to be together. Maybe we *could* be happy together.

"What's that smile about?" I ask as we move in a gentle slow dance around the floor.

"Today went well."

"Yes, it did." I grin. "You're welcome, for my brilliant idea."

He spins me and pulls me into his chest. His arm goes behind my back, trapping me there. "It was a very good idea, Francesca."

"Frankie," I remind him.

"Frankie," he repeats in my ear, his voice close enough to give me goosebumps.

Movement from the corner of my eye catches my

attention. I glance over and spy Charlie making a covert stabbing motion with her finger. I can't figure out what she's trying to tell me, but I'm not about to yell over everyone's heads.

Dante spins me again at arm's length. He's just about to bring me back in when he stiffens, his smile dropping. There's a soft touch on my shoulder.

"Mind if I cut in?" a man asks. It's a voice I'd know anywhere.

A voice I hoped I'd never hear again.

I turn toward the man and freeze, my limbs becoming stone. Charlie is pushing her way through the crowd, her face frantic, and I realize what she'd been trying to tell me. But she stops in her tracks when she sees that she's too late.

"Who the hell are you?" Dante asks, wrapping a possessive arm around my waist.

Rico doesn't notice or doesn't care. He smiles in his easy way and holds up a hand, pointing to the wedding band on his finger as he boldly claims my gaze.

"I'm her husband."

Dante and Frankie's story continues in
Broken Vow…

I thought the past was behind me… but becoming Mrs. Bellanti put a target on my back.

My husband isn't a gentle man.
And God knows he isn't the sharing type.

Rico's announcement has dropped a bomb into my marriage.

Both of them.

I never thought I'd see Rico again.
Never thought Dante would ever have to know.
Seeing the way he looks at me now, as though I'm just another problem to be handled?
It's breaking my heart.

I thought I was in love once before.

I swore I wouldn't make the same mistake twice.

But falling for a Bellanti was far worse than a simple mistake...

Find out what happens in Broken Vow.

PAIGE PRESS

Paige Press isn't just Laurelin Paige anymore...

Laurelin Paige has expanded her publishing company to bring readers even more hot romances.

Sign up for our newsletter to get the latest news about our releases and receive a free book from one of our amazing authors:

Laurelin Paige
Stella Gray
CD Reiss
Jenna Scott
Raven Jayne
JD Hawkins
Poppy Dunne
Lia Hunt

The Bellanti Brothers

Dante

Broken Bride

Broken Vow

Broken Trust

ABOUT THE AUTHOR

Stella Gray is an emerging author of contemporary romance. When she is not writing, Stella loves to read, hike, knit and cuddle with her greyhound.

Made in the USA
Monee, IL
13 November 2021